Florence T. Donnell

Moneymaking and Matchmaking

Or New York in 1890

Florence T. Donnell

Moneymaking and Matchmaking
Or New York in 1890

ISBN/EAN: 9783744739955

Printed in Europe, USA, Canada, Australia, Japan

Cover: Foto ©Andreas Hilbeck / pixelio.de

More available books at **www.hansebooks.com**

MONEYMAKING

AND

MATCHMAKING;

OR,

New York in 1890.

Comedy in Five Acts

BY

FLORENCE T. DONNELL.

NEW YORK:
WILLIAM R. JENKINS,
851 & 853 SIXTH AVENUE.
—
1891.

CHARACTERS.

DANIEL THURMAN. A new man from the Wild West, entirely out of place in a civilized community.

JEREMIAH GRABALL. The greatest man in Wall street.

PERCY GRABALL. Aristocratic scion of a plebeian stock. Very little brains, and any quantity of clothes.

J. BLACKSTONE VAN HUCKSTER. Knickerbocker aristocracy, has lived in London.

T. RUSHINGTON FLASHEM. The Chicagoan of the present and the American of the future.

CHARLEY TATTLETON, of Boston, lives at the clubs. A great deal of family and any quantity of leisure.

JACK BADMINTON. A muscular dude. Excels in fox hunting.

LORD EUSTACE FITSHUBERT FLUSHINGTON. Authentic English nobleman, with summer seat at Ring-Ring on the Hudson.

COUNT CRISPINO DE LA COMARE. Authentic Italian Count, descendant of the illustrious Barberini family.

TACITURN STIFFNECK. High-toned and deep-draughted English butler; has a low opinion of American culture.

TOM TRIMMINS. District messenger boy. Lively and enterprising, already well up in stocks.

CHARACTERS—(Continued.)

Mrs. KETCHUM. New York mamma, determined and enterprising. Employs refined and subtle methods.

Mrs. HUNTER. Another of the same sort, but cruder and more abrupt.

BLANCHE KETCHUM. Unique and improbable New York girl.

ETHEL HUNTER. Ordinary and highly probable New York girl.

Mrs. BLACKSTONE VAN HUCKSTER. Knickerbocker aristocracy, sixteen quartering, and unnumbered coats of arms, aspires to a peerage.

Mrs. RUSHINGTON FLASHEM. Practical Chicago widow, goes in for money.

Miss ACRITONIA GUSHINGTON. Many times disappointed, but still hopeful.

SUZETTE. French maid, with Irish accent and American views of life.

Act I.—Matches.

Act II.—A Great Match.

Act III.—The Money Making.

Act IV.—The Money Losing.

Act V.—Matched.

MONEYMAKING

AND

MATCHMAKING.

ACT I.

Parlor in Mrs. Ketchum's house, Fifth Avenue, between 42d St., and the Park. Doors, r. and l. Large door, or curtained opening c. f. leading to conservatory. Table l. c, mantelpiece, arm-chairs, etc., right.

SCENE I.

STIFFNECK, *dusting, and arranging furniture in a grumbling manner.*—Did h'ever h'any one see such h'an 'ouse, h'and they calls this style h'in h'America a h'expectin h'of the butler to h'answer the door bell, h'and they h'a talkin so much h'about h'English fashions. Why the first thing they do when they sets h'up 'ousekeepin h'in h'England h'is to 'ire h'a buttons to do h'all the work, so the butler may take 'is h'ease, h'and h'enjoy is h'ale, h'and tea, (*bells ring.*) Ring! ring h'away, h'I'll teach h'em good form, h'and let that h'Irish, French, h'American vixen Suzette h'answer the bell 'erself. She liked to scratch my h'eyes h'out for jist tryin to look h'over 'er shoulder h'at 'er bank-book. HI dont believe she's got h'anything worth showin laid h'away h'any 'ow. H'and then h'a peaceable h'Englishman might h'as well 'ave dynamite h'under 'is roof h'as a woman h'of all them three nationalities.

(*Enter Suzette, d. l.*)

SCENE II.

SUZETTE *and* STIFFNECK.

Suzette.—Shure, and what do 'ye mean Misther Stiff-neck a' throubling of people like that answerin of your bells, when faith my hands are full, and flowin over with work a gettin the young ladies ready for the afternoon reception.

Stiffneck.—H'I thought may be h'it 'ud be the post-man, h'and you 'ah be a likin to see h'if 'e 'ed h'a brought me one of them letters from my rich h'uncle h'in the h'old country, you 're h'always a' h'askin h'about.

Suzette.—Uncle indade, is it ye say? I don't believe you 've got one. Why, shure it's a district messenger boy h'askin for the madame.   •

Stiffneck.—Well! why don't you go tell my lady. You cant be 'a h'expectin me to do your work h'up stairs too.

Suzette.—Dont you be giving me none of your sass. (*Aside.*) But shure, and I wonder if he really has a rich uncle, or if it's only his English humbug.

(*Exit Suzette.*)

———

SCENE III.

Stiffneck.—She h'aint worth bein civil to, for h'I don't believe she's got one farthin to 'er name. But h'I wonder what the district messenger 's h'a comin for h'at this hour. H'I'll call 'im h'in, h'and see. (*Goes to door and calls.*) This way, my lad, h'in 'ere.

(*Enter Tom Trimmins, district messenger boy, d. l.*)

SCENE IV.

STIFFNECK *and* TRIMMINS.

STIFFNECK.—H'I say, my lad, what brings you h'in 'ere, so h'early this h'afternoon.

TRIMMINS.—I aint your lad, nor nobody else's, I'm Tom Trimmins, number 21,050 of the District Messenger Company, and I come from Mr. Jeremiah Graball, the greatest man in Wall street, with a message for Mrs. Ketchum, No. — Fifth Avenue, and I've been waiting ten minutes out in the entry with no chair to sit on.

STIFFNECK.—H'a message from Mr. Jeremiah Graball, the great stock broker, but 'ave you h'any kind h'of h'an h'idea what there might be h'in it?

TRIMMINS —Jim Mullins says he thinks it's a love affair, the old boss was in such a hurry and excitement about it. But he's a soft 'un is Jim Mullins; it's stocks, I know it's stocks. No one in America is ever in a hurry about anything but stocks. But I say, Johnny, you 've lost something.

STIFFNECK.—H'and what may I 'ave lost, young man?

TRIMMINS.—H'only your haches. H'only your haches. Rats! I say Rats!

STIFFNECK, (*aside.*)—The low h'American brat.

(Enter Mrs. Ketchum.)

———

SCENE V.

MRS. KETCHUM, STIFFNECK *and* TRIMMINS.

MRS. KETCHUM.—Well! have you a message for me? Let me see. (*Putting on her glasses.*) For Mrs. W. Howard Ketchum?

TRIMMINS.—There aint no double Howard about it. It's just for Mrs. Ketchum; that's all there is on the envelope.

MRS. KETCHUM, *impatiently.*—Give it to me anyway. (*Aside.*) That Jeremiah Graball always will be ill bred and vulgar, as if anyone could live in New York society now, without a double name. (*Opens envelope and reads; shocked and astonished.*) Oh! Ah! My! Stiffneck what are you standing, staring for? Give me a pen and ink right away.

STIFFNECK.—Very well, my lady.

(*Mrs. Ketchum seats herself at table and writes hastily.*)

TRIMMINS, *aside.*—Chesnuts! I say chesnuts! Stocks must have tumbled.

STIFFNECK, *aside.*—H'I dont 'alf like the looks h'of this. That low brat must 'a been right, h'and she's lost money.

MRS. KETCHUM. — Here take this to Mr. Graball's office, as quick as ever you can go. Have you the change for the cars?

TRIMMINS.—Yes, the company gives me that, but I say the hansoms travel much quicker. Oh! if you 'ed send me in a hansom I 'ed take it in a giffy

STIFFNECK.—Yes, my lady, the 'ansoms do go very quick.

MRS. KETCHUM, *aside.*— Stiffneck looks at me so strangely, I wonder if he thinks I can't afford it. (*Handing Trimmins money.*) Go, now, take a hansom and be quick.

TRIMMINS.—You may bet I'll be off now. (*Aside.*) A ride in a hansom. What a jolly lark that 'ill be ; but aint she a high 'un. Oh! my eye!

(*Exit Trimmins.*)

SCENE VI.

MRS. KETCHUM *and* STIFFNECK.

MRS. KETCHUM.—You may go, Stiffneck, but wait, when Mr. Graball calls, ask him into the little sitting-room, and let me know instantly.

STIFFNECK.—Which Mr. Graball, my lady ?

MRS. KETCHUM.—Old Mr. Graball, of course. Young Mr. Graball doesnt count while his father lives. (*Aside.*) For I know the old man keeps him on a short allowance.

STIFFNECK.—Very well! my lady. (*Aside.*) This h'all looks h'aweful queer. May be h'I'll 'ave to be seekin h'another place before night.

(*Exit Stiffneck.*)

SCENE VII.

MRS. KETCHUM, *reading.*

" Mrs. Ketchum,

" Dear Madame,

" Much to my surprise, there was a sharp tumble in the Match Trust this morning. Just as we had made our arrangements to start an up movement, we began to feel the presence of a big bear operator in the market. Now, as I do not think there is anyone else in the combine who would dare to undertake operations of such magnitude, I will not conceal from you that all my suspicions have centered on your Western friend, Daniel Thurman, whose boldness, large command of money and well known enmity to trusts, would explain the whole mystery, if indeed there were not deeper motives for such a manœuvre on his part. Those motives, I think I will be able to make clear to you. Then it is urgent that I should see you as soon as possible, as the loss on your stock is already considerable, amounting to no less than $175,000 and if the present condition of the market continues, it will be necessary to put up heavy margins to-morrow. I shall try to be up at your house by six o'clock to see what can be done, but should you wish to see me sooner, let me know by messenger boy. Meanwhile I am, yours very sincerely,

" Jeremiah Graball."

One hundred and seventy-five thousand dollars. Good heavens! and that would only leave me twenty-five thousand to live on, and Blanche not married yet. Oh! what a miserable, wretched woman I am with the prettiest girl in New York for a daughter, and she the most perverse, ungrateful, cold-hearted, cruel creature. Her poor mother worked to death, yes, literally worked to death, giving entertainments, worrying morning, noon, and night, trying to make $200,000 do the duty of two millions, and fretting herself to the bone, just to find that unreasonable child a husband who would do credit to us both. And to think that she might have Daniel Thurman, the greatest catch in New York. A man who can make millions as quick as he has, and to think that she won't have him and that she treats him abominably, cruelly. Cruel, why, I call it inhuman.

(*Looking at letter again.* Oh! was there ever such an unfortunate, wronged woman. Everybody cheats me, everybody imposes upon me. But what does old Graball mean by saying he knows Thurman did it, and can explain his motives, and that he too has some arrangement to propose. Oh! they both evidently want something from me, may be I can make a bargain with them yet.

(*Enter Mrs. Hunter, d. r.*)

SCENE VIII.

Mrs. KETCHUM *and* Mrs. HUNTER.

Mrs. Hunter.—What has kept you so long, Mary Ann?

Mrs. Ketchum.—Gracious goodness! don't call me by that horrid name. Stiffneck might hear you, and it's such a vulgar name in England.

Mrs. Hunter.—I beg your pardon, but old school habits, you know. (*Aside.*) I really believe she's putting on airs because her daughter is so much talked about ; as if I didn't remember when she used to come to Pa's country grocery, a little barefooted girl, and was mighty glad to catch poor Ketchum, the bookkeeper, though she did lead him a life. (*Aloud.*) Ah! you 've just received a letter, is it one from the guests you expect this afternoon? I hope it's not from Mr. Thurman to say he can't come. (*Aside.*) And after all the money I've spent at Blueleaf's on Ethel's dress.

Mrs. Ketchum.—No, it's from Mr. Graball.

Mrs. Hunter. Young Mr. Graball, and is he not coming either? (*Aside.*) Such a delightfully silly young man, and with such lots of money.

Mrs. Ketchum, *aside.*— How the woman wearies me, as if she could get either of them for her ugly, gawky, little minx of a girl, while my Blanche is still unmarried. (*Aloud.*) Oh! it is not a social note at all, it is a business communication about some stock in the match trust which Mr. Graball sold for me at the top of the market, and he tells me here of the profit I have made on the decline.

Mrs. Hunter.—A match trust, goodness heavens! and I have no stock in it. What will become of my poor daughter?

Mrs. Ketchum.—Oh! you don't understand me, Mrs. Hunter, I mean a trust in matches.

Mrs. Hunter.—A trust in matches! I should think so, who hasn't a trust in them for sooner or later!

Mrs. Ketchum.—Oh! I mean matches such as you light the gas with.

Mrs. Hunter, *with a sigh of relief.*—Ah!

(*Enter Blanche and Ethel, d. r.*)

———

SCENE IX.

BLANCHE, ETHEL, Mrs. KETCHUM *and* Mrs. HUNTER.

Mrs. Ketchum.—Ethel, my dear. how lovely you look!

ETHEL.—Yes, is'nt it too awfully stunning, it's one of Blueleaf's latest. Just see, there's more than ten dozen brass buttons and yards, and yards of gold braid on it.

MRS. HUNTER.—Yes, Ethel gets all her gowns there. There's no place in New York to compare to it. Why; have you seen the pages they have now at the doors? They're just too lovely with their striped green and yellow silk hose, and scarlet velvet jackets, with birds of paradise's tails on the shoulders for epaulettes, and the cutest, little crushed strawberry satin polo caps, with Rhinestone aigrettes and peacocks' plumes standing straight up in them. Oh! the combination is just too artistic for anything.

BLANCHE.—I should think the poor little fellows would look like grotesque monkeys escaped from some travelling menagerie.

MRS. KETCHUM.—Oh! Blanche, my dear, how can you? Why the Queen herself patronizes Blueleaf's establishment.

MRS. HUNTER.—And it's a real pleasure even to get his bills. They're so covered over with coat-of-arms that I put them on the top of my card basket every time.

ETHEL.—But, mamma, there's one thing I don't like about the establishment. Do you remember that rainy day we went there in a shabby cab, how awfully they snubbed us, and were only civil when Mr. Stronghand, the manager, came forward and recognized us. It was the first time I ever was glad to see him, for he's so rough, he almost knocks me down every time he tries on a cloak.

(*Enter Stiffneck.*)

SCENE X.

STIFFNECK, Mrs. KETCHUM, Mrs. HUNTER, BLANCHE and ETHEL.

Stiffneck.—My lady, h'it's Mr. Graball, h'and h'I h'asked 'im h'into the little sitting room, h'as you bid me.

Mrs. Ketchum.—Very well, Stiffneck, go tell him I will be there instantly. (*Aside.*) He has come before he received my note. He must be anxious. May be all will be won instead of lost. (*Aloud.*) Mrs. Hunter, will you keep the dear girls company in my absence and receive in my place if I am not back in time.

Mrs. Hunter, *aside.*—Mrs. Hunter! She does that just to keep me at a distance. (*Aloud.*) Oh! trust me to take the best of care of the dear children.

(*Exit Mrs. Ketchum.*)

———

SCENE XI.

Mrs. HUNTER, BLANCHE and ETHEL.

(*Blanche and Ethel near fire-place on the right, Mrs. Hunter seated near table, l. c.*)

Mrs. Hunter.—Oh! don't mind me, girls, I shan't be in your way. I'm going to read Tolstoi, he always interests me so much, and just think Anna Karenina is too lovely for anything. That description of her mother's death is so awfully pathetic, and the account of her third marriage is too beautiful for anything. Oh! there can't be too many weddings for me, I just love them. But there, you mustn't interrupt me, for I want to follow the story closely.

(*During the following scene, Mrs. Hunter nods over her book till she falls fast asleep.*)

BLANCHE.—What book is that you have, Lizzie?

ETHEL.—Oh! don't call me Lizzie, if Ma were to hear you. To be sure I was christened Elizabeth after an aunt of Pa's, whom we expected to leave me some money, but she died, and didn't, after I 'ed been called twelve years by that hateful, ugly name. Now, wasn't that nasty, horrid mean. But English fashions were just coming in then, so Ma changed my name to Ethel from a proper sense of pride. But this book, Ma says there's no harm in my reading it, if I don't let any of the fellows know I've even heard of it. It's "The Slip of the Lip" they talk so much about. They say it's perfectly scandalous, and I know I'm going to have just the nicest time reading it.

BLANCHE.—If you will take my advice, Ethel, you will throw it in the fire, for it is sure to be insufferably stupid. It is only people who are conscious of a lack of real talent who appeal to notoriety through scandal.

ETHEL.—But you, what are you reading?

BLANCHE.—Oh! it's Ibsen's dramas, I was just trying to begin them. Mamma wants me to read them, and I always try to please her in anything reasonable.

ETHEL.—Oh! Blanche, do you know why she wants you to read them. It's because they are serious, awfully serious, and she thinks it will please Mr. Thurman.

BLANCHE.—If I thought that, I would never look in the book again.

ETHEL.—How can you, Blanche? I think he's just splendid. You can't deny that he's stunning fine looking anyway.

BLANCHE.—Why should I deny it? What is Mr. Thurman to me.

ETHEL.—There now, don't pretend, doesn't everybody say you're going to marry him next spring, and what a catch you 'ill get. If you could only see his new house at Lenox; Ma has seen it. She says the mantelpiece is just wonderful, and cost a fortune in itself, and then he owns the best parterre box at the Opera. He bought it from old Tangent when he failed last winter. I'm sure though I don't envy you, anyway, for whatever Ma may say about it, he isn't my style. But you will ask me to be bride's maid, wont you, for there will be a splendid turn out at the wedding.

BLANCHE.—Don't talk in that way, Ethel. Oh! it is all a torture and a shame, this life we girls lead. It is unnatural and unmaidenly in a glare of publicity from our childhood, ignorant of the world, we are expected to cope with it at every turn, and affect a knowledge which would be disgraceful to us if we possessed it, and is ridiculous when we do not. I hate and despise all these men with their insolent presumption and their low familiarity. Oh! I hate and despise them all, and I will never marry one of them. Never, there!

ETHEL.—Why, Blanche, what a little fury you are, you fairly take my breath away, but you can't say Mr. Thurman is familiar. Why he is as grand and stately as I am sure an English duke must be, and besides he never says more than five words together, unless you excite him, and then his eyes flash, and he talks just as wildly as you do.

Blanche.—I am sure, Mr. Thurman is not at all like me.

Ethel.—Well! let us leave him alone, we will both hear enough of him from our Mas to-night anyway, and all this talk has knocked out of my head just what I wanted to tell you. Do you know I received such a sweet, lovely letter last night from Count Crispino de la Comare. Oh! such a charming letter, I am sure no American could have written it.

(*Enter Stiffneck.*)

SCENE XII.

BLANCHE, ETHEL, Mrs. HUNTER *and* STIFFNECK.

Stiffneck.—H'are you h'in, Miss, h'or will you be h'out?

Blanche.—Oh! we are in, Stiffneck. Miss Hunter and I are both in. (*Mrs. Hunter wakes up with a snort.*) Mrs. Hunter also.

Shiffneck, *throwing the door open.*—Show the gentleman h'in, John. The young ladies 'ave both concluded to be h'in.

(*Enter Percy Graball.*)
(*During the following scenes Stiffneck stands in front of door and announces each visitor before he enters.*)

SCENE XIII.

PERCY GRABALL, Mrs. HUNTER, BLANCHE *and* ETHEL.

Mrs. Hunter.—Oh! Mr. Graball, I'm just delighted to see you. These girls were just saying that you are always so entertaining. Do try, and wake them up, for they've been 'most asleep.

PERCY.—And did they say I was entertaining? Oh! that is awfully good of them. Nobody ever said that before.

BLANCHE.—Did you see Lakmé last night, Mr. Graball, and is the music really as pretty as they say?

MRS. HUNTER, *aside to Ethel.*—What makes you let that forward girl monopolize all his attention. Can't you say something, and he such a catch, too.

ETHEL.—Oh! Mr. Graball, have you been to the Casino lately. They say the scenery is just too lovely for anything.

PERCY.—I didn't look much at the scenery, but they have five new girls in the chorus, regular stunners. Why, one of them is over six feet tall, and has a staring red and white complexion.

MRS. HUNTER.—It's all paint, besides I can't endure those tall women.

ETHEL.—He! he! he! (*Aside.*) Isn't Ma too cute for anything.

MRS. HUNTER.—Ethel, my child, you have a very bad cough, I really do think you must have caught cold at Mrs. Toploftus' tennis party last week. Oh! Ethel does so adore out-door sports, Mr. Graball.

PERCY.—Really, I think they are awfully jolly myself.

BLANCHE.—Did you see the race between Fantastic and Flippant at Jerome Park yesterday? I do so like a race where there are only two horses and a dead-heat. Then one can be pleased for both of the brave creatures and need not be sorry for either.

PERCY.—But you don't win on either, when they are both quoted even before the race. Why, Jack Grabbem took Flippant and I took Fantastic, and we were neither of us a bit the better for it.

MRS. HUNTER, *aside to Ethel.*—Don't you see how she is monopolizing him, can't you say something?

ETHEL.—But I do hope you were more lucky on some of the other races.

PERCY.—No, I lost a pile on Fantom in the Downtown Stakes, and as Pa only gives me an allowance, and after the pile I lost at Sheepshead last summer, he said he wouldn't pay another penny for me, so I had to let go and knock under.

MRS. HUNTER, *aside.*—I have suspected this all along, and the old man will live forever. (*Draws her chair away from Percy; aloud.*) Ethel, my dear, come here, there is something wrong about the sleeve of your dress.

STIFFNECK, *announcing.*—Mr. Charles Tattleton and Mr. John Badminton.

(*Enter Badminton and Tattleton.*)

SCENE XIV.

MRS. HUNTER, BLANCHE, ETHEL, PERCY, BADMINTON, TATTLETON *and* STIFFNECK.

BADMINTON.—I caught Charley at the club and hauled him right up here.

TATTLETON.—It did not require Badminton's intervention to remind me that I might have the pleasure of meeting you this afternoon, Mrs. Hunter, and the young ladies too, but where is Mrs. Ketchum?

Mrs. Hunter.—Mrs. Ketchum asked Ethel and I to help her receive, and as she is unavoidably detained, she thought you might excuse her for a few minutes, the more particularly as it is only an informal five o'clock. I am sure we will do our very best to entertain you.

Tattleton.—And I am sure you will succeed most charmingly, Mrs. Hunter.

Mrs. Hunter, *aside.*—He knows everybody, he is a most valuable acquaintance, and then that rich uncle of his may die any day. (*Aloud.*) Ethel, my dear, don't you heard Mr. Tattleton is speaking to you?

Ethel.—I didn't hear him, Mamma. (*Mrs. Hunter frowns with warning gesture.*) Oh! I really beg your pardon, Mr. Tattleton.

Mrs. Hunter.—Oh! the dear child is so absent minded. She's a real Boston girl, Mr. Tattleton, she delights in nothing but learned books.

Tattleton.—And what have you been reading lately, Miss Ethel?

Ethel.—Oh! I was just reading the "The Slip—"

Mrs. Hunter.—The "Sleeping Beauty," Mr. Tattleton, a learned German work on comparative myths, and fairy stories, particularly relating to that beautiful tale which has delighted us all in our childhood.

Badminton.—Oh! I say, Mrs. Hunter, have you heard of Windbaggin's new invention, it's just glorious. A kind of bicycle with a trapeze on top. It's for two fellows, one of them works the bicycle while the other exercises on the trapeze in the open air. They say Central Park 'ill be full of 'em next year. I told Windbaggin I'd order three of 'em right off.

BLANCHE.—But are you not afraid, Mr. Badminton, that people will laugh at you?

BADMINTON.—No, they never laugh at anything in New York when it's the fashion. Besides Windbaggin says they 'ill be all the rage in London next spring, and then they 're sure to take here.

TATTLETON. — A strange municipal government we have which prohibits innocent street bands, and yet would permit horses to be frightened and harmless pedestrians killed by such a machine as that.

STIFFNECK, *announcing.* — Miss Acritonia Gushington.
(*Enter Miss Acritonia.*)

—

SCENE XV.

MRS. HUNTER, BLANCHE, ETHEL, MISS ACRITO-NIA, PERCY, BADMINTON *and* TATTLETON.

ACRITONIA.—Oh! Mrs. Hunter, I'm just charmed to see you looking so well, but I do hope that dear Mrs. Ketchum is not ill.

MRS. HUNTER.—Oh! no, thank you, Miss Acritonia, she will be here directly,

ACRITONIA.—And the dear girls, how lovely they look, but between us two, don't you think they are dressed too gaily for their age, for they are only little chits, you know, little chits.

MRS. HUNTER, *aside.*—The mean, envious thing. (*Aloud.*) But here, Miss Acritonia, is a friend whom you will be glad to see, and who will be delighted to see you.

Acritonia.—Oh! Mr. Tattleton, how could you treat me so, you naughty, naughty man, it's ages since I've seen you. I do believe you just live at the club.

Tattleton.—I beg you to believe, Miss Acritonia, that I would be totally incapable of neglecting you for the most attractive club in the world, but I have been away for six months trying to cheer up my poor old uncle, Mr. Pogwoggon in Florida.

Acritonia.—Oh! that dear Mr. Pogwoggon, and has the Florida climate improved his health?

Tattleton.—I can hardly say so, Miss Acritonia, he was looking very poorly when I last saw him.

Acritonia.—Oh! the poor dear man. (*Aside.*) They say he is worth millions, and will leave them all to Tattleton. I'd like to be sure of it. It doesn't do to be reckless at my age.

Tattleton.—By the way, Miss Acritonia, have you heard from your venerable aunt, Mrs. Dinever, lately? She was a perfect picture when I saw her last, with her beautiful white hair, and her stately old time manners.

Acritonia.—Oh! I am sorry to say, Mr. Tattleton, that she is failing fast. I— I am afraid that she will not be spared to me through the winter.

Tattleton.—Oh! indeed, I am so sorry. (*Aside.*) If I could only believe her, but these old maids are so artful.

Stiffneck, *announcing.*—Mrs. Flashem and Mr. T. Rushington Flashem.

(*Enter Mrs. Flashem and T. Rushington Flashem.*)

SCENE XVI.

Mrs. HUNTER, Mrs. FLASHEM, BLANCHE, ETHEL, ACRITONIA, FLASHEM, TATTLETON, BADMINTON *and* PERCY.

Mrs. Hunter.—Oh! Mrs. Flashem, I am so glad to see you, we were all talking about you, and wondering why you were so late.

Mrs. Flashem.—Oh! that was real kind of you, but it's all the fault of that son of mine. He's never on hand when he's wanted. How do you do, Miss Acritonia, how are you, girls, you're both looking lovely.

Flashem.—Now, Ma, don't be unreasonable, when a fellow has as many irons in the fire as I have, he never has much time for any one thing. Why, I was up at five o'clock this morning, took a galop round the park, noticed that the bridle path was badly paved, and thought of a new composition made of cork, and other stuff to try on it, will submit to Park Commissioners to-morrow; rode on to 150th Street, and looked at some lots a fellow wants to make me swallow. Found too many rocks in 'em; no go. Then rushed home, wrote a hundred letters, or so, telephoned to my agent down town to buy a ship load of cork seized at the Custom House and advertised for sale. Then spent most five minutes at breakfast and was down town in less time than it takes to tell it. Worked like a beaver there to get off before six o'clock. So, you see, Mrs. Hunter, I was as good as my word, anyway.

Mrs. Flashem.—You hear how that boy talks, he seems to think that no one else ever has anything to say. Tom, you go and entertain the young people, for I have something to tell Mrs. Hunter, and Miss Acritonia too, for I am sure she will enjoy the humor of it (*aside*) and spread it abroad.

(*Mrs. Flashem, Mrs. Hunter and Miss Acritonia l. the rest, r.*)

Mrs. Flashem.—It's all about that stuck-up Mr. Van Huckster.

Acritonia.—Oh? what is it? I should so like to know.

Mrs. Hunter.—Oh! I do hope she has not entrapped that poor innocent Lord Flushington.

Mrs. Flashem.—Lord Flushington, indeed! I should think not. After her ignominious failure with Lord Raspin, it's about time she 'ed given it up. Why don't you know the bans were published, and it was just six days from the wedding, when Raspin found out his lovely, young bride was not as richly endowed as he thought, so he said he 'ed rather have none of it, and retreated abruptly, and Mrs. Van Huckster is still hunting for some forlorn English peer willing to take her.

Mrs. Hunter, *with anxiety.*—And has she found him?

Acritonia.—Oh! do tell us all about it.

Mrs. Flashem.—No, but I've found somebody who knows all about her, and that family of hers she talks so much of; Knickerbocker aristocracy indeed! Why, she is no more Knickerbocker aristocracy than you or I.

Mrs. Hunter.—I beg your pardon, Mrs. Flashem, but my maternal grandfather was Petrus Van Herbarsten one of the oldest Dutch settlers.

Acritonia.—And my grand-father, Colonel Gushington, was own cousin to Jonas Van Stranghausen, so famous in our early colonial annals, and my mother's—

Mrs. Flashem.—Never mind, ladies, if you tell me all about your families, I'll never have time to tell you anything of Mrs. Van Huckster's before she arrives. Well! her father kept a little green grocery down in Baxter Street, and she used to wait on the counter; and Van Huckster, who do you suppose he was? Why, a street vender, a man who went around with a hand-cart, and bought up green fruit from the West India steamers, and then dragged the cart all over the town to sell it. Some people say he had a horse in the cart, but I don't believe it, I think he dragged it himself.

Acritonia.—Yes, indeed, that would account for the aristocratic gout that crippled him in his old age.

Mrs. Hunter.—And they put on such airs afterward.

Mrs. Flashem.—The street boys called him Huckster. His own name must have been something worse, for he adopted that as an improvement. Well! in the course of trade, he visited the Baxter Street green grocery, met the fair daughter of the house, fell in love with and married her.

Mrs. Hunter.—Is it possible ; and that was the way Mrs. Van Huckster began life.

Mrs. Flashem.—Yes, Mr. Van Huckster was never in any better business than that, but he speculated in vacant lots, and made piles of money. And then they added the Van to their names, got an assortment of coats-of-arms, and went in for aristocracy.

Acritonia.—So, he made all his money in vacant lots, did he? No wonder Mrs. Van Huckster considers landed property so aristocratic.

(*Badminton and Flashem detach themselves from group on the right and advance towards fore-ground.*)

BADMINTON.—Do, like a good fellow, give me a point on stocks, for I've been awful hard up since the ten thousand dollars I lost on the great high-kicking match between Briggs and Riggs.

FLASHEM.—Give you a point. Take my advice in one thing, Jack, points in stocks from a smart fellow like me, are about the sharpest-edged weapons any young man can receive and are sure to stab him every time.

TATTLETON, *coming forward.*—Do you know what they were saying down at the Union Trust Club this afternoon. Why, that old Jeremiah Graball took Mrs. Ketchum in on matches to-day, and made her lose thousands and thousands of dollars in a few hours.

FLASHEM.—Took her in on matches! Great stars! I did'nt know there was a man living could do that. Why, she spends her whole life studying them.

TATTLETON.—Studying matches, I didn't know she had any time for such things.

BADMINTON.—Oh! he means sparking, the spoons and that kind of thing.

FLASHEM.—Yes, trying to spark matches that never will go off.

TATTLETON.—But these weren't that kind of matches, they were the sulphurous sort.

FLASHEM.—Sulphurous, I should say so ; that was what any match the old lady put her hand to was sure to be. I'll wager that her son-in-law will find the sulphur red hot and burning every time.

TATTLETON.—Oh! you know I mean the match trust, and it's a serious thing, too.

FLASHEM.—Yes, from what I've heard I can well believe it. But those cork pavements took up my whole day, and I had hardly a minute to spend at the Exchange. But come, tell me all about it.

STIFFNECK, *announcing.* —Mrs. Van Huckster and Mr. J. Blackstone Van Huckster.

———

SCENE XVII.

Mrs. HUNTER, Mrs. VAN HUCKSTER, Mrs. FLASHEM, BLANCHE, ETHEL, ACRITONIA, FLASHEM, VAN HUCKSTER, PERCY, TATTLETON *and* BADMINTON.

STIFFNECK, *as Van Huckster passes him.* — 'and H'e thinks that looks like h'an h'Englishman.

MRS. HUNTER.—Oh! I'm delighted to see you, Mrs. Van Huckster.

MRS. FLASHEM.—And I, too ; I'm just delighted.

ACRITONIA.—And I too, dear Mrs. Van Huckster, we are quite strangers to one another now.

MRS. VAN HUCKSTER.—And I, too, am pleased to see you all, but it was really so warm this afternoon, that I almost gave up all idea of coming. (*Aside.*) These dreadful, noisy people, why can't they have some English repose of manners, (*Aloud.*) But where is Mrs. Ketchum ?

MRS. HUNTER.—Oh ! she will be here in an instant. (*Aside.*) I wonder if this disagreeable woman is really worth cultivating anyway.

ACRITONIA, *aside.*—She's looking around to see if Lord Flushington is here.

VAN HUCKSTER.—But have any of you fellows, seen Flushington to-day?

TATTLETON.—No, but I met De la Comare at the Windsor this afternoon, and he said he had an appointment with Flushington, and that they would be up here towards six o'clock.

VAN HUCKSTER.—It's most six now, it's almost time he was here.

FLASHEM.—I say, Van Huckster, what makes you care so much for that stupid Englishman; I don't think I ever saw such a blockhead in my life.

TATTLETON.—Besides, nobody knows who he is.

BADMINTON.—He's the poorest hand at billards I ever saw, and drinks like a fish. For my part, I like little Cormarini, or whatever you call him, a deal better; there's some fun in him.

VAN HUCKSTER.—Why do I like him, for his truly English repose of manner, his admirable self-control, his extensive knowledge of the ways of the world, and for that remarkable good form which distinguishes him, and makes him a suitable companion for a gentleman.

(*Enter Mrs. Ketchum, followed by Jeremiah Graball.*)

SCENE XVIII.

Mrs. KETCHUM, Mrs. HUNTER, Mrs. VAN HUCK-
STER, Mrs. FLASHEM, Miss ACRITONIA,
BLANCHE, ETHEL, JEREMIAH GRABALL,
PERCY, FLASHEM, VAN HUCKSTER, TATTLE-
TON *and* BADMINTON.

Mrs. Ketchum, *aside to Graball.*—I can scarcely believe what you tell me about Mr. Thurman. It seems hardly possible that he would resort to such a manœuvre to force my consent to his marriage with my daughter. But, never mind, Mr. Graball, he shall gain nothing by it ; I will speak to Blanche in your dear boy's behalf. I am sure he has misinterpreted her words ; youthful feelings are so susceptible ; but I will put it all right. (*Aloud.*) Ladies I do hope you will excuse my absence; a little unavoidable detention caused by a trifling matter which Mr. Graball has most kindly, successfully, I dare even say triumphantly arranged for me, with profit to us both ; is it not so, Mr. Graball?

Graball.—I hope so, and I believe so, Mrs. Ketchum.

Mrs. Van Huckster.—Oh! my dear Mrs. Ketchum, I should so like to have a talk with you. It is about both our children.

Mrs. Ketchum.—Such a topic would charm me, Mrs. Van Huckster, but I fear we will have to postpone it till to-morrow morning when we will have a nice, quiet corner to ourselves. (*Aside.*) Does she think I am going to let Blanche marry her great ninny of a son when I have millions in my grasp.

Stiffneck, (*announcing.*)—Lord Eustace Fitzhubert Flushington and Count Crispino de la Comare.

(*Enter Flushington and de la Comare.*)

SCENE XIX.

Mrs. HUNTER, Mrs. KETCHUM, Mrs. FLASHEM, Mrs. VAN HUCKSTER, Miss ACRITONIA, ETHEL, BLANCHE, LORD FLUSHINGTON, COUNT DE LA COMARE, FLASHEM, JEREMIAH GRABALL, PERCY, TATTLETON *and* BADMINTON,

Mrs. KETCHUM.—Oh! Lord Flushington, I am so glad to see you, what has made you so late? We had almost given you up.

FLUSHINGTON (*starts*).—Given me up! (*Recollects himself.*) Oh! you overwhelm me, Madame, you really do, but I came as soon as I could.

Mrs. KETCHUM.—And we are all so pleased to see you, and you too, Count de la Comare.

COMARE.—Oh! Madame, your charming kindness puts me beside meselve. Vil you permit me to kiss your lofely hand?

Mrs. KETCHUM (*aside*).—He has such courtly manners, any one could see he was a nobleman.

Mrs. VAN HUCKSTER.—Oh! Lord Flushington, won't you sit down here, I want to ask you so many questions about some London customs.

Mrs. HUNTER.—Oh! yes, do, Lord Flushington.

Mrs. KETCHUM.—Count de la Comare, you are so gallant, will you not entertain the young ladies, I am sure they are longing to hear your descriptions of your beautiful country.

COMARE.—Oh! I vil be so delighted, Madame. (*Joins group on right.*)

Mrs. Ketchum (*aside*).—Those Italian noblemen are never rich, but they give distinction, and I'd like to see something about his attention to Blanche in Low Down Antics next Thursday. Nothing would help us more in this crisis, but I wonder why Mr. Thurman does not come, I'm beginning to be anxious.

Stiffneck, *announcing.*—Mr. Daniel Thurman.

(*Enter Thurman*).

SCENE XX.

Mrs. KETCHUM, Mrs. HUNTER, Mrs. VAN HUCKSTER, Mrs. FLASHEM, Miss ACRITONIA, BLANCHE, ETHEL, THURMAN, FLASHEM, VAN HUCKSTER, JEREMIAH GRABALL, PERCY, BADMINTON, TATTLETON, LORD FLUSH-INGTON, and COUNT DE LA COMARE.

(*Stiffneck still in front of door*).

Mrs. Ketchum.—Oh! Mr. Thurman, I'm so glad to see you. We were all wondering what kept you, and my Blanche was just saying that your absence spoilt all our afternoon.

Thurman.—And did Miss Blanche say that?

Blanche.—How can I remember such trifles?

Mrs. Ketchum, *aside to Thurman.*—Oh! don't mind the child, she's shy, and then when they feel deeply, you know how young girls are.

Mrs. Flashem.—Oh! come, Mr. Thurman, and sit down here, I have a lot of questions to ask you.

Mrs. Hunter.—Oh! no, do come here first, Mr. Thurman, I want you to come, hear something Lord Flushington is telling us, it is so entertaining. (*Aside.*) Does that brazen-faced Chicago widow think she can catch him. When a woman has had one rich husband, I think it is a downright shame for her to try, and get another. I call it monopoly, I do.

Thurman, *aside, looking at Blanche.*—She never gives me one friendly glance, one kind word. Why should she who is so gentle to others, be so harsh to me?

Flashem.—But, I say Thurman, come here, we fellows want to ask you something about stocks.

J. Graball.—Oh! don't ask him about stocks, or he will talk philosophy to you. He thinks everything is governed by philosophy, even the stock market. (*Aside.*) I must get him in a corner, and learn the secret of that rise in wheat.

Badminton.—Oh! but Mr. Thurman won't you tell us how the cowboys out West manage to keep on bucking horses?

Mrs. Flashem.—Oh! yes they say you were a cowboy once yourself, Mr. Thurman. Oh! how lovely and romantic.

Thurman.—It is quite true, madame, I was a cowboy once, but it was only for a few months, when I could get nothing else to do. For the rest, it was a wild, but not unpleasant life. (*Aside.*) She prefers to talk to that chattering fool Tattleton, rather than even look at me.

Mrs. Flashem.—And what kind of men are the cowboys, anyway, Mr. Thurman?

Thurman.—Oh! good enough fellows, very much like any other men.

Van Huckster.—Oh! you don't mean to say they are like the fellows one meets at the Club?

Mrs. Van Huckster.—Oh! you don't mean to say that if we were to see one of them here, he could be mistaken for one of our young society men?

Thurman.—Here, I do not see why not; but if you were to see both men on horseback, you could never make such a mistake; never!

Mrs. Van Huckster, *aside.*—What a low subject of conversation. (*Aloud.*) Did you enjoy your trip in Europe last summer, Mr. Thurman?

Thurman.—Yes, I enjoyed it very much, though I scarcely took a fashionable tour, but traveled around the country, and through the popular quarters of the great cities, visiting the schools and manufactories.

Mrs. Van Huckster.—Oh! didn't you find the country in England awfully charming.

Thurman.—Yes, it certainly is very pretty, but I think I felt more at home on the continent.

Van Huckster.—Why, I should think a New Yorker would find everything very strange on the continent, it is not a bit English there.

Tattleton.—But I am anxious to know what would strike an intelligent observer like you most on a first European visit; I mean the chief difference between Europe and America.

Mrs. Flashem.—Oh! yes do tell us, I'm just expiring to know.

Badminton.—They're an awful slow set over there, aint they?

THURMAN.—No, they are not slow. I think they are moving just as rapidly, in one direction, as we are in another; for while they are striding towards democracy with a startling impetus, we are rushing into a pseudo aristocracy, an oligarchy of unscrupulous wealth and presumption, with a recklessness which appals all intelligent and patriotic observers, who love their country, and have hoped for it a glorious and useful future.

MRS. VAN HUCKSTER, *to Mrs Hunter.*—How low to talk against aristocracy in a New York drawing-room.

MRS. HUNTER.—But, he is so rich, you know, no rules need exist for him; but, I think he must intend to run for Congress, or he wouldn't profess such ridiculously democratic sentiments.

MRS. KETCHUM, *aside.*—If this continues much longer I'll never get to the point.

(*Motions to Stiffneck, and speaks to him in a whisper.*)

STIFFNECK, *throws open doors, and announces.*—My lady is served.

(*General stampede of guests for the dining-room. In their haste, they jostle, hustle and almost fall over one another.*)

BADMINTON.—We're going to have a feed at last.

FLASHEM.—I thought it was going to be a dry entertainment. The old woman is smart enough for such sharp practice.

PERCY, *to his father.*—You look mighty jolly, Pa.

GRABALL.—Yes, my boy I've cornered the matrimonial market, and your future is assured.

*(Mrs. Van Huckster and Mrs. Hunter both try to seize on
Lord Flushington. After many futile efforts on his part
to escape, he is overpowered, and offers an arm to each of
them. Mrs. Ketchum and Thurman bring up the rear,
and when all the others are gone, and they reach the door,
she pauses.)*

SCENE XXI.

Mrs. KETCHUM and THURMAN.

Mrs. Ketchum.—I would so like to speak to you for
a few minutes in private, Mr. Thurman, it is about a
matter which concerns the happiness of my poor
daughter.

Thurman.—Miss Blanche's happiness. Oh! I would
do anything, I would dare anything, even her displeas-
ure, if I could have the proud consciousness of render-
ing her, the smallest, the most insignificant service.
Oh! Mrs. Ketchum, you do not know how I love your
daughter.

Mrs. Ketchum, *aside.*— At last! *(Aloud.)* I have long
suspected it, Mr. Thurman, and something Mr. Graball
has just been telling me has made those suspicions
certainties. I am sure you are not ignorant of the
interest I have had lately in matches.

Thurman.—Do you mean the match trust which
declined to-day; I am very sorry to hear it. But will
you permit me to arrange your difficulties. I will
esteem it a privilege, I assure you.

Mrs. Ketchum.—Ah! I knew that after you had sent
the stock down more points than I could carry at, you
would come to my assistance.

THURMAN.—I send the match stock down, because I knew you held it. Could you believe me capable of such base conduct, Mrs. Ketchum?

MRS. KETCHUM.—Ah! do not suppose that I bear any malice against you. All's fair in love, or war. You know how reluctant I am to part with my only child, and might as an impatient lover, use any stratagem to force my consent.

THURMAN.—Stratagem to force your consent! What do you mean, Mrs. Ketchum?

MRS. KETCHUM, *aside.*—He is not as smart as I thought, but he can't mean to back out now. (*Aloud.*) But Mr. Thurman, my maternal feelings, my reluctance to part with my Blanche shall never be allowed to interfere with her happiness.

THURMAN.—Ah! Mrs. Ketchum, if I could believe she had for me the least, I will not presume to say tender sentiment, but sympathy, or esteem, I would deem myself the happiest of men, if——

MRS. KETCHUM, *eagerly.*—If what, Mr. Thurman?

THURMAN.—If I could be sure she would willingly accept me. If I could be sure it would not break her heart to marry me.

MRS. KETCHUM, *aside.*—It will be more difficult than I thought. (*Aloud.*) Of that I can convince you easily, Mr. Thurman. Go to the dining-room, and tell Blanche I would like to see her, then wait outside in the conservatory till I call you, and you may ask her yourself. You will see what she will say.

THURMAN.—Oh! how can I thank you?

(*Exit Thurman.*)

SCENE XXII.

Mrs. KETCHUM.

Mrs. Ketchum.—I must be quick with that foolish child, a sudden shock is my only hope. I came near spoiling everything just now by my deliberate methods.

(*Enter Blanche.*)

———

SCENE XXIII.

Mrs. KETCHUM and BLANCHE.

Mrs. Ketchum.—Oh! Blanche, my child, my heart is broken, I hardly dare to tell you, you poor dear.

Blanche.—Why, what is it, Mamma? dont cry like that.

Mrs. Ketchum.—Oh! it is a dreadful thing to tell you, but we are ruined my little Blanche, Mr. Thurman has just told me so.

Blanche.—And what can Mr. Thurman know of our affairs, Mamma.

Mrs. Ketchum.—Why don't you know, haven't you seen this long time, that he's in love with you, and you, you cruel girl, you have treated him, the best match in New York with scorn, and contempt. And he seeing no other prospect of obtaining your hand, has employed a stratagem which I must say does the greatest honor to his intelligence.

Blanche.—And that stratagem, I can assure you, Mamma, that whatever it is, it will be unsuccessful.

Mrs. Ketchum.—Unsuccessful! and would you see your poor mother ruined, a pauper, compelled to beg her very bread, unable to give a single entertainment, and obliged to give up her box at the opera. What would life be worth to me then ? Why, do you know if our accounts were settled to-night, we would not have $25,000 to live on, and I with my poor health.

Blanche.—And you would wish me to marry a man who has reduced us to such a position.

Mrs. Ketchum.—If I were asking you anything unreasonable ; but Mr. Thurman is a man no woman need be ashamed to take into society, he is really distinguished looking when he has on a dress suit, and as he seldom opens his mouth in general company, he is not likely to say anything to compromise us. Oh! if you would only marry him, your poor mother could die in peace and tranquility.

Blanche.—But tell me what was it, this mean scheme, this base stratagem, you speak of.

Mrs. Ketchum. — Well, a few weeks ago, old Mr. Graball induced me to take stock in a new match trust he was starting, and I, thinking of your future ventured most of our little fortune, and M. Thurman hearing of this, with his usual acuteness, determined to force my hand, so he someway got hold of a quantity of stock, which he threw on the market this morning, and provoked such a decline that we are completely at his mercy.

Blanche.—And you ask me to marry a man who would do such a base thing.

Mrs. Ketchum.—But my goodness me! if you don't, where will we get the money to put up the margins to-morrow ? Unless you would prefer to borrow it from old Mr. Graball, who has promised it if you consent to marry his son Percy. And there is no time to be lost in either case. But I will not disguise it from you; in my opinion there is no comparison between the two men. Why ! Percy's father keeps him on a very short allowance, and he has never made a dollar in his life, and never will, and the most talented woman couldn't make him appear much, while Mr. Thurman is one of the most successful speculators in Wall Street. You see yourself there is no comparison. Ah ! Blanche, my little Blanche, do decide, for your poor Mamma's sake.

BLANCHE.—And is there no escape, no way to save me from such a degradation.

MRS. KETCHUM.—Degradation ! what words you use.

BLANCHE.—Mamma, is there no way to save us ?

MRS. KETCHUM.—No; and I will go tell Mr. Thurman that you reject his proposals; that you scorn his proffered help; that you are willing that your poor mother should go down broken-hearted, and poverty stricken to a miserable grave. (*Coughs violently.*) There! there is my cough come back again. But you, what do you care whether I die, or not, nor how soon.

BLANCHE.—Mamma, does it really hurt you?

MRS. KETCHUM.—Hurt me, I should think so, I feel as if I was just going to die this minute.

BLANCHE.—And would it make you happy if I said I would marry Mr. Thurman. If it would, I will do it.

MRS. KETCHUM, *suddenly recovers.*—Happy! I should think so; but if I call him now, you won't say anything ugly to him; and if he asks you if you consent willingly, you will say yes ?

Blanche.—Yes; I will say anything, if you only do not look as you did just now.

Mrs. Ketchum, *opens door, and calls joyously.*—Mr. Thurman, Mr. Thurman.

(*Enter Thurman.*)

SCENE XXIV.

Mrs. KETCHUM, BLANCHE and THURMAN.

Mrs. Ketchum.—I told you Mr. Thurman that if you would but permit me to plead your cause with my daughter, she would consent.

Thurman.—And do you really consent to be my wife, Miss Blanche, willingly, freely.

Blanche, *looking at her mother.*—Yes, willingly.

Thurman.—Oh! if you only knew how proud I am of your confidence, your esteem, I dare not say love, but even that I hope to win, if you only knew——

Blanche.—Spare me your protestations, Sir, there—— there is some one coming.

(*Enter all the guests d. c. f. from the dining room.*)

SCENE XXV.

Mrs. KETCHUM, Mrs. HUNTER, Mrs. VAN HUCKSTER, Mrs. FLASHEM, Miss ACRITONIA, BLANCHE, ETHEL, THURMAN, FLASHEM, JEREMIAH GRABALL, PERCY, BADMINTON, TATTLETON, LORD FLUSHINGTON and COUNT DE LA COMARE.

Mrs. Ketchum, *aside.*—I must not leave him a chance to slip out, nor that headstrong girl either. (*Aloud.*)

My friends I take this opportunity to make the first announcement of the engagement of my daughter to Mr. Daniel Thurman. I know you will all offer us your best wishes, though I am sure you will sympathise with me in what I cannot help regarding as a bereavement.

Mrs. Van Huckster.—I am sure I am very much pleased, and wish you all the good fortune you deserve. (*Aside.*) The silly girl, when she might have had my Blackstone.

Mrs. Flashem.—Oh! I'm sure I never was so pleased in my life. (*Aside.*) The great blockhead, I could tear his eyes out.

Mrs. Hunter.—My dear Mrs. Ketchum, you must know how pleased I am. (*Aside.*) After all I've spent, and all I've done to get him for Ethel.

Graball.—Mrs. Ketchum, you're a very smart woman, and deserve anything.

Acritonia.—I do so love weddings. When will it come off? (*Aside.*) Did anyone ever see anything like the luck of these girls?

Tattleton.—I am sure you will have a most distinguished son-in-law. (*Aside.*) He has neither family, nor education; but nothing goes down here but money.

Badminton.—I hope you won't forget to invite me to the wedding, Mrs. Ketchum. (*Aside.*) I do hope it 'ill be in the evening, and that they will have a good supper, those wedding breakfasts are mean shams.

Ethel.—Oh! do have a grand wedding, Mrs. Ketchum; they're too splendid for anything. (*Aside.*) When I get married, I mean to elope.

Lord Flushington.—Will you receive my best wishes, madame. (*Aside.*) What piles of money that man must keep in his safe.

Count de la Comare.—Will you permit me to congratulate you, madame, and your lofely daughter; and still more, the happy bridegroom. (*Aside.*) He has a very fine head of hair, but he doesn't put enough pommade on it.

Percy.—Mrs. Ketchum, I'm sure I wish you the very best of luck, and hope you will be awfully happy. (*Aside.*) I didn't want to get married anyway, and then she's drawn the line on Pa, and that's just glorious.

Van Huckster.—I hope you will all be awfully happy. (*Aside.*) If the girl had no better taste than to take that common fellow when she might have had me, she's not worth regretting.

Mrs. Ketchum, *aside.*—Now I can rest in peace, I have done my duty as a mother.

Thurman, *aside.*—How I love her, I wonder if there is any man on earth happier than I am.

Blanche, *aside.*—What have I done to deserve this degradation. Oh! how I despise him.

(*Curtain.*)

ACT II.

SCENE I.

(*Parlor in the house of Daniel Thurman.*)

STIFFNECK, *making a show of dusting and arranging furniture in a leisurely kind of way.*—H'I cleared h'out h'of Mrs. Ketchum's mighty quick h'after that day h'of the fall in the Match Trust. But h'I think h'I'm safe 'ere h'anyway, h'and h'as Mrs. Thurman keeps twenty-five domestics, h'I h'aint troubled with h'anything to do, but h'announce the visitors. H'I wish h'I could h'only know what to think h'of that girl Suzette. She dresses very fine, but h'all the women h'in h'America dress stunnin, whether they 'ave the money to pay for it h'or not. H'I think h'I'ed better not decide too soon, for h'is she French, h'American, or h'Irish, h'it's h'all risky h'anyway, for the women in h'all them countries 'avent a proper sense h'of their h'own h'inferiority. They thinks themselves the h'equals h'of men, h'and h'acts h'as if they were their superiors. H'I think h'I'ed better not try h'it, for she boxed my h'ears last night when h'I h'attempted to kiss her, h'as an h'openin wedge, h'and we h'Englishmen likes to do h'all the beatin h'ourselves. H'and maybe she h'aint got nothing h'in the bank, h'after h'all, so h'I think h'I'ed better not venture.

(*Enter Suzette.*)

SCENE II.

SUZETTE and STIFFNECK.

Suzette.—And shure and madame 'ill be in here directly, and you aint got nothing arranged.

Stiffneck.—H'and do you h'expect me to do h'all the work h'in the 'ouse. (*Aside.*) H'I wonder h'if h'it's worth while being civil to 'er.

Suzette, *aside.*—Maybe I'd better not say anything more to him, for he had another one of those letters yesterday. (*Aloud.*) Has Mr. Thurman gone down town yet?

Stiffneck.—H'I should think so, 'e went hours h'ago. H'and is this what they calls an 'oneymoon h'in h'America. They h'aint been married six weeks, h'and my lady 'as a sick 'eadache h'every morning, h'and never shows 'erself till hours h'after 'er 'usband's gone down town; then she h'appears towards one h'o'clock h'entirely well h'again, h'and dressed to kill, h'and receives h'a lot h'of visitors, h'and goes h'out towards four h'o'clock, h'and comes h'in h'again h'at six with h'another sick 'eadache, h'and 'er 'usband h'eats h'is dinner h'alone, h'and h'after waiting h'a while for my lady to make 'er h'appearance 'e goes h'off to the club, h'and h'as soon h'as 'e's h'out h'of the 'ouse, my lady comes down h'again got h'up to kill, h'and goes h'off to the h'opera, h'or some h'other place where there's 'ighjinks, h'and then they both comes h'in, h'in the small hours of the morning, h'and the h'instant my lady sets foot h'in the 'ouse, she 'as h'another sick 'eadhache, h'and shuts 'erself h'up. H'and is this what they calls h'an 'oneymoon h'in h'America?

SUZETTE.—And shure and what better would you want. Didn't everybody envy Miss Blanche when she married the rich Mr. Thurman, and hasn't she the purtiest corner house on the Avenue, just stocked from top to bottom with French pictures, carved wood, Chinese monsters, and things, and hasn't she the place in Lenox with the fifty thousand dollar mantelpiece, and a cottage at Bar Harbor, and a splendid box at the opera, and lots and lots of things besides, and didn't Mr. Thurman give her the longest and thickest diamond necklace in New York, and hasn't she already spent ten thousand dollars on her dresses. Madame Mulligan's boy told me so meself yisterday, and what more could a rasonable woman expict?

STIFFNECK.—H'I can h'understand that she might be satisfied, but h'I should think that when 'e 'ed a married a poor girl, h'and you know she was poor, for the h'old missus was burst h'up that day by the fall h'in the Match Trust. H'I say that when 'e'ed h'a married h'a poor girl for 'er beauty, 'e 'ed naturally like to see something h'of 'er. H'I call h'it h'a cheaten h'a man h'out 'o 'is money's worth, h'I do.

SUZETTE.—And if he did marry her for her beauty, and shure what would he want to see her for, doesn't he hear her looks talked about in all the papers, and oughn't that be enough for him; shure, and I don't know what more h'ed be wantin, for if they niver see one anither, how kin they quarrel? All the divorces come from married people seein and knowin too much of one anither, but there I hear some one coming. It must be the madame; so quick, fix things, do.

(Enter Blanche d. r.)

SCENE III.

BLANCHE, SUZETTE and STIFFNECK.

Blanche.—Here Stiffneck is a letter, I would like you to take to my mother's.

Stiffneck, *aside.*—These h'Americans will never know h'anything h'about style. Ten men h'in the 'ouse, h'and h'a h'expectin h'of the butler to take a letter. (*Aloud.*) H'and can't h'I send h'it by h'a messenger my lady?

Blanche.—You may send it any way you like, only I want it to go quickly.

(*Exit Stiffneck.*)

Blanche.—And you, Suzette, go round to Madame Mulligan's, and see if she cannot finish my white gauze dress in time for the opera to-night.

(*Exit Suzette.*)

SCENE IV.

BLANCHE.

Blanche.—What a wretched and irrational thing life is! and I who thought myself so superior to all these people, and now— now I am more contemptible than any of them, for I spend this man's money just— just to fill up the the time, and keep from thinking. And he, when I think of what he did, and that they made me marry him, I hate him, and ah! how I hate, how I loathe and despise myself. But how could a man who would do such a thing, find such proud, and tender looks, such gentle and manly ways. But I will not see him again, I will not.

(*Enter Stiffneck, d. r.*)

SCENE V.

BLANCHE and STIFFNECK.

STIFFNECK —H'it's young Mr. Graball my lady. 'E seems very h'excited, h'and strange my lady, h'and 'as some great 'orrid thing h'in 'is 'and, h'and h'insists h'upon bringin h'of h'it h'in.

BLANCHE.—Oh! ask him in, Stiffneck, he always is a little strange.

STIFFNECK, *throws open door, and announces.*—Mr. Percy Graball.

(*Enter Percy Graball.*)

(*Stiffneck continues to stand in front of door during the following scenes.*)

———   •

SCENE VI.

BLANCHE and PERCY.

(*Percy carries a bucket and broom painted in brilliant colors, and tied with huge bows of ribbon of many shades, and Mr. Graball in large letters on the bucket.*)

PERCY.—Oh! Mrs. Thurman, I wanted to know if you 'ed be so awfully kind as to let me leave this here till to-morrow morning. It's a little favor they gave all us fellows at Mrs. Litherford Jumbleton's luncheon around the corner, and in trying to take it home in the coupé, the broom handle crashed through one of the windows, and I know Pa will be raspin mad. I couldn't throw it into the street, as my name's painted on it, so I brought it in here, and will you be so awfully nice as to let me leave it, till I can send a messenger to fetch it away.

BLANCHE.—Oh! certainly, Mr. Graball, there are no objections to it's remaining here, but what a queer thing to give for a favor.

PERCY.—Do you think so, Mrs. Thurman? why, it's nothing to what we got the other night at Mrs. Fitzmaurice Friskam's German. Why, each of us fellows received a huge box of soap decorated all over with American flags and little jingling bells. And Mrs. Friskam said the flags were to mark the soap as the national emblem, and the bells were to attract the attention of the ladies. And Flashem, who was there, said Mrs. Friskam was an awful cute woman. But what are you laughing at? I can tell you it was no joke to carry 'em.

BLANCHE.—I was only thinking Mrs. Friskam shows a strange kind of wit in her selections.

PERCY.—Anyway, they were awful heavy. The idea of expecting a fellow to carry anything as heavy as that, unless it was a cane.

BLANCHE.—But what did the young ladies receive?

PERCY.— Oh! they got the best of the bargain, they had fishing nets and fishing hooks that caught in every fellow's hair as they moved around, and then the married women got match-safes, with lots and lots of bows on them, to brighten them up, Mrs. Friskam said.

BLANCHE.—I think I must cultivate Mrs. Friskam's acquaintance, she seems to be the only woman in New York who makes a rational selection of favors.

PERCY.— Oh! but you ought to have seen the brooms stacked up in the center of Mrs. Jumbleton's lunch table, all strung with bows and bouquets, and every fellow had a bucket in front of him, as a champagne cooler, all wreathed around with flowers, and Mrs. Jumbleton said that was a Greek luncheon, and it was too jolly for anything, for each of us fellows got his full quart bottle of Veuve Cliquot.

Stiffneck, *announcing.*—Mr. John Badminton.

(*Enter Badminton.*)

SCENE VII.

BLANCHE, PERCY and BADMINTON.

Badminton.—Oh! I'm awfully glad to see you Mrs. Thurman, and you, too, Percy old boy. You have an awfully jolly place here, haven't you, and you're looking just lovely.

Blanche.—And you too are looking well, Mr. Badminton, the country air seems to have agreed with you.

Badminton.—Yes, I tell you, Mrs. Hurlington Hallum has a jolly, snug place down there, at Braxedo, and we fellows just went it.

Percy.—Were there many jolly girls down there?

Badminton.—Girls! I don't know, but there were lots of stunning horses, and we went fox hunting every day.

Blanche.—Ah! the poor foxes, how could you be so cruel?

Badminton.—Don't you worry about the foxes, Mrs. Thurman, there wern't any of 'em anywhere about; but we hunted 'em all the same. We were at it from morning till night, and had such jolly luncheons out on the grass. But the last hunt was an awful fluke, for we came to a wire fence miles long, with no way round it. It was too high for the horses to walk over, and we couldn't pull it down, for it had spikes sticking out all over it ; so we turned back, and went home.

BLANCHE.—But couldn't you leap over it ?

BADMINTON.—Leap over it! why it was fully two feet high.

PERCY.—But I thought the American horse couldn't be beat for leaping.

BADMINTON.—Neither can he, there is no animal in the world can beat the American horse at leaping. But the trouble is that he has such a quick unruly way of shooting up into the air, that he's almost sure to leave his rider behind him.

STIFFNECK, *announcing.*—Miss Acritonia Gushington, and Mr. Charles Tattleton.

SCENE VIII.

BLANCHE, Miss ACRITONIA, TATTLETON, PERCY and BADMINTON.

TATTLETON.—I met Miss Acritonia out on the stoop, and she was kind enough to permit me to escort her in. What a lovely home you have, Mrs. Thurman. (*Aside.*) How overcrowded with things these parvenu's houses are.

ACRITONIA.—Oh! my dear Mrs. Thurman, you look just too lovely for anything. (*Aside.*) I really do believe she's beginning to fade already.

Blanche.—Have you heard anything lately from your old Aunt, Mrs. Dinever, Miss Acritonia?

Tattleton, *quickly.*—Oh! she is worse than ever, Mrs. Thurman. I've just been asking Miss Acritonia out on the stoop, and she says she can't last through the winter, poor, dear old lady.

Blanche.—Indeed! I am very sorry to hear it.

(*Tattleton, Percy, and Badminton form group on the right, Blanche and Acritonia, left.*)

Acritonia.—Have you seen anything of Mr. Tattleton's dear pleasant old uncle, Mr. Pogwoggon?

Blanche.—I havn't seen him lately; he's dyspeptic, you know, and thinks cold weather injures him, so he goes early to Florida every season.

Acritonia, *aside.*—Florida and dyspepsia. If one of them doesn't kill him, the other surely will.

Blanche.—Ah! now I think of it, I did see him last week at the Wagner concert, and as he sat erect, and attentive for four hours, I think he must be very well indeed.

Acritonia, *aside.*—Four hours of Wagner. Ah! he can't survive that long, unless he's made of iron.

Stiffneck, *announcing.*—Mrs. Rushington Flashem, and Mr. T. Rushington Flashem.

————

SCENE IX.

Flashem.—How do you do, Mrs. Thurman, and you too, Miss Acritonia. How d'ye do, boys. You've got a stunning roost in here.

Mrs. Flashem.—Oh! yes, it's just lovely, and I tell you, your curtains make a stunning show from the street, but fine as they are, I think I can beat you on 'em. Oh! I wish you could just see my front parlor, I've had it rigged up as an Egyptian room, for you know the Moorish, Pompeian and Renaissance rooms have been done to death, so I've had mine fixed up in Egyptian style, and Tom has sent to Egypt to get a genuine mummy of one of the Pharoahs to put in the bay window.

Acritonia.—So people can see it from the street.

Mrs. Flashem.—Yes, of course. and then everyone will ask whose house it is. For that purpose it will be better than the handsomest Sèvres vase, but I wish you could see the lovely Egyptian gown I'm having made, to receive in.

Acritonia.—At Bluefeaf's?

Mrs. Flashem.—No, at Madame Bridget Mulligan's, she's French you know, and we Chicago people are not so crazy about English things as you New Yorkers. But I wish you could see my dress, it's just lovely, what there is of it.

Blanche.—And how is it made, Mrs. Flashem?

Mrs. Flashem.—Oh! you don't suppose I'm going to give away my ideas, but I'll tell you something about it. It's all slashed up on one side to show the foot.

Acritonia.—I didn't know a Chicago woman ever wanted to show her foot.

Mrs. Flashem.—And why not, when it has a fine boot on it.

BLANCHE.—Continue, Mrs. Flashem, and tell us how the rest of the dress looks.

MRS. FLASHEM.— Oh! it's just lovely, it takes so little to make it, and then it shows the neck, and arms so beautifully.

TATTLETON, *aside to Badminton.*—I should think a woman as fat as that, would never want to show her neck and arms.

BADMINTON, *aside to Tattleton.*—And why not ; one can't see too much of a good thing.

FLASHEM.—Did you notice how low-spirited Thurman looked to-day. I tell you he must have been losing at stocks.

TATTLETON.—Maybe he has some trouble with his pretty wife. They don't seem over affectionate. Why, you never see them together.

BADMINTON.—Yes, he spends all his evenings at the Club now, and mercy knows, it isn't lively there.

FLASHEM.—A smart fellow like Thurman get the dumps about a woman! nonsense! Women! women! I tell you there are too many of 'em already in America. The market's overcrowded and overstocked with 'em. They do nothing but spend, spend, and don't add one dollar to the national wealth. I'd export a lot of 'em, and then there 'ed be more money to go round, and a deal less mischief.

TATTLETON.—But you may marry some day yourself, Flashem.

PERCY.—Yes, you may get spoony some day yourself.

FLASHEM.—Spoony, nonsense, no man of the present day believes in such a thing as love. Marry, humbug! I shan't marry till I'em eighty or ninety, and too old to speculate. I tell you no fellow has nerves strong enough to run a wife, and the stock market at the same time. But this is what I might do. If some fellow were to appear with a stunning ability for catching the boys and running trusts, and combines, and if the same fellow were to throw a daughter on the market, I might bid her in, in order to get points from the father, that is if I were sure he had uncommonly strong family feelings; for otherwise he might trick me, make me pan out, and keep me on a pension just to show how smart he was. Ah! marriage, even under such attractive circumstances, is a risky business, and T. Rushington Flashem, 'll look a good many times before he leaps. Besides I can marry Ma to the speculator, and then I will get all the points without any risk, for there is one person no man in America will cheat, and that's his wife,—she's such a convenient cover for property in a case of fraudulent bankruptcy. But I never half liked the idea of Daniel Thurman for a step-father. He's too attractive a fellow, and too much affection would spoil the only rational use a marriage could be put to.

TATTLETON.—Now, I think of it, I did hear some gossip at the club about Thurman having lost a pile on the flutter in wheat.

BADMINTON.—But a few millions more or less, what difference can that make to Dan? Mrs. Thurman will give swell dinners all the same.

(*Percy and Badminton go up towards background.*)

FLASHEM, *to Tattleton.*—Now since those boys are gone, I can tell you what it is. It's more serious than you think, it's old Graball taking his revenge on Thurman for getting Mrs. Ketchum out of his clutches when he cornered her on matches, and thought he had her dead. Thurman's the smartest fellow of the two, but maybe he's one of those queer survivals who believe in love. If he's got that kind of nonsense in his head, he'd better pan out right off and knock under, for old Grabb's as cool as a cucumber.

Tattleton.—He has no cultivation whatever, and not even the most rudimentary education.

Flashem.—Nonsense! he has forty millions.

Stiffneck, *announcing.*—Mrs. Van Huckster and Mr. J. Blackstone Van Huckster.

(*Enter Mrs. Van Huckster and Mr. J. B. Van Huckster.*)

SCENE X.

BLANCHE, Mrs. FLASHEM, Mrs. VAN HUCKSTER, FLASHEM, VAN HUCKSTER, PERCY, TAT-TLETON, BADMINTON and ACRITONIA.

Mrs Van Huckster.—Your house is really very beautiful. Mrs. Thurman, it has quite an English look.

Van Huckster.—But don't you find it very hot in the city in December, Mrs. Thurman?

Blanche.—Oh! not at all, I even find it pleasant in September.

Mrs. Van Huckster.—Oh! we never leave the country till after Christmas. It is so homelike to take the

Christmas dinner in the great family hall, with the portraits of one's ancestors hanging round, and a big blazing log fire to make it cheerful.

Van Huckster.—Then the tenants think it's so awfully jolly to have us there.

Tattleton, *aside to Flashem.*—Tenants, why they have only a cottage with ten rooms in it at Seabright, and five acres around it, with not even a tree in them.

Badminton.—Yes, but they'd rather freeze than come into the city before the first of January.

Percy.—I should think they'd get the dumps down there, with nothing to keep 'em company but the great howling ocean.

Flashem.—Oh! we know it's all sham, but it pays in New York.

Acritonia.—But doesn't this arrangement of staying in the country so late suit the English climate better than ours?

Blanche.—Yes, the English winter climate is much milder than ours.

Mrs. Van Huckster.—The English climate is just lovely I think the London atmosphere in November is just too sweet for anything, it's so delightfully solid and substantial.

Mrs. Flashem.—But isn't this dodge of staying in the country till you're frozen stiff a new idea?

Badminton.—And the climate couldn't have changed in the last five years, you know.

Van Huckster. — But if it is necessary that the American climate should be changed in order to become English, it will be, you know.

STIFFNECK, *announcing* — Mrs. Hunter, Miss Ethel
Hunter, Lord Eustace Fitshubert Flushington, and
Count Crispino de la Comare.

SCENE XI.

BLANCHE, ETHEL, MRS. HUNTER, MRS. FLASH-
EM, MRS. VAN HUCKSTER, MISS ACRITONIA,
FLASHEM, VAN HUCKSTER, LORD FLUSH-
INGTON, COUNT DE LA COMARE, PERCY,
TATTLETON and BADMINTON.

BLANCHE.—Oh! I am so glad to see you, Mrs. Hunter,
and dear Ethel, too.

MRS. HUNTER.—And I, I've just been dying to come
around to see you before, but couldn't. (*Aside to Ethel.*)
Ethel, don't you waste your time on that della
Cormarini, but hold on to Lord Flushington; can't
you see that Van Huckster's woman is dying to grab
him?

TATTLETON, *aside*.—Where have I seen that Italian
before?

VAN HUCKSTER.—Oh! Lord Flushington I want to ask
you a question about cross-country riding.

BADMINTON.—Yes, we all know you Englishmen are
such good judges of field sports, I'm sure you can tell
us.

FLUSHINGTON.—Oh! I'll be awful glad to oblige you,
I'm sure.

VAN HUCKSTER.—We were disputing as to whether a
horse would show his best speed on a fine smooth road,

such as you have in England, or on a rolling country with short green turf.

FLUSHINGTON.—Oh! I should think that would depend upon how hotly he was pursued by the bai—

BADMINTON, and Van Huckster. Pursued ! !

FLUSHINGTON, *aside.*—Curse my stupidity. (*Aloud.*) What was I saying, pursued; why, pursued by the dogs of course.

BADMINTON.—Oh! is that the way they do it in England? They let the fellows out first, and then send the dogs after them. Oh! that would be a jolly idea down at Braxedo, where we have no foxes, and the cursed beasts of dogs run in every direction, and lead a fellow such a race.

COUNT DE LA COMARE, *to Ethel.*—Oh! my adored, if you would but listen to me.

ETHEL.—Oh ! yes, but I will listen to you some other time, when Ma isn't looking.

COMARE.—And you vil, how you call it here, elope wid me to-morrow, from Mrs. Ketchum's ball, and ve vil be married, and go away to sunny Italy, to my beautiful home.

ETHEL.—Oh! yes, indeed I will, but on one condition.

COMARE.—And vat is that condition, my adored.

ETHEL.—That you will send me to-morrow morning that photograph of your castle in the Appenines, you promised me.

COMARE.—Oh ! I vil send it my beautiful adored, I vil send it to-morrow evening. (*Aside.*) Time to get it taken.

ETHEL.—No, I must have it before midday, or I won't go.

COMARE, *aside.*—She wants to verify it. (*Aloud.*) Oh! you are a real American girl.

(*Enter Thurman, d. r.*)

SCENE XII.

MRS. HUNTER, MRS. FLASHEM MRS. VAN HUCK-STER, MISS ACRITONIA, BLANCHE, ETHEL, THURMAN, FLASHEM, VAN HUCKSTER, LORD FLUSHINGTON, COUNT DE LA COMARE, PERCY, TATTLETON and BADMINTON.

STIFFNECK, *as Thurman passes him.*—Well h'if 'e 'asn't brass to present 'imself like that h'in my lady's reception without being h'announced.

Chorus of the women, with the exception of Mrs. Van Huckster who preserves a stately frigidity.)—Oh! Mr. Thurman, we are so glad to see you. Oh! Mr. Thurman, we're just delighted, it's just too sweet to see you once again. You're quite a stranger; why don't you come to see me, *etc., etc.*

MRS. VAN HUCKSTER, *aside.*—And to think that Blanche Ketchum married that common man, when she might have had my Blackstone. Oh! these people make me so nervous, they have no English repose of manner.

FLASHEM.—Oh! do tell us about the stock market. Ma hauled me up here before I could get half a bite at it this morning.

Thurman.—Oh! there was rather an excited market, but that will hardly interest these ladies.

Mrs. Flashem.—Oh! yes it will, Mr. Thurman, we Chicago women are all interested in stocks.

Mrs. Hunter.—Oh! yes, we poor mothers have to keep track of such things.

Acritonia.—Oh! yes, I'm sure it would be most interesting and beautiful, as you would describe it.

Mrs. Van Huckster.—Yes, do tell us how English consols were.

Thurman.—You will excuse me ladies. I know it is only a polite desire to please and entertain me, that causes you to wish to listen to such dry subjects. (*In a whisper to Blanche.*) Won't you speak to me, Blanche, won't you even look at me.

Blanche.—And what would you have me say ; before all these people, too.

Thurman.—But when they are gone away, may I remain?

Blanche.—You can do as you like, it is your own house.

Mrs. Flashem.—Oh! do you know, Mr. Thurman, what Tom saw about you in the newspapers? Why, that you were going to run for Congress out West. Is it true?

Thurman, *smiling.*—About as true as such things usually are in the newspapers, that is there is a little truth in it. Six years ago when they were trying to elect an honest and patriotic man to the presidency, with enough intelligence to see the difficulties, and dangers of the situation, and enough integrity to combat them, I did what service I could.

FLASHEM.—Oh! yes I heard you were a famous stump speaker.

MRS. VAN HUCKSTER, *aside.*—Stump speaker, why can't they say he spoke from the hustings, as cultivated people should.

THURMAN.—I am inclined to think that my services were overrated, but whatever ability I possessed I endeavored to use, for every day convinces me more, and more that no time is to be lost in stemming the moral corruption which is gangrening the vital forces of this country, and is making its political life an ever spreading fountain of demoralization, and its social life an aggregation of grotesque shams.

FLASHEM.—But I say, Thurman, tell us about your running for Congress, for who is interested in the politics of his country, excepting from a personal point of view.

THURMAN.—Oh! it's a short story, after the presidential campaign was successfully concluded, the majority of the inhabitants of the town where I was born wanted me to run for Congress from their district. Circumstances then compelled me to decline. They renewed their offer the other day, and I suppose that was the origin of the paragraph.

MRS. FLASHEM.—Oh! but you won't consent, you won't take dear Blanche away, just at the beginning of the ball season.

FLASHEM.—And you won't go away just when the stock market is getting lively.

THURMAN.—I have not decided yet, the decision will depend upon the choice of another.

MRS. HUNTER.—Oh ! you mean Blanche; Blanche, dear Blanche, don't consent to bury yourself in the wild West. Don't go to that horrid Washington. (*Aside.*) It's too exclusively a matrimonial market. Poor Ethel would have no chance there.

PERCY, *to Badminton.*—I say, Badminton, it's getting awfully slow here. Let us be off to the Casino.

BADMINTON.—No, let us go up to the Athletic Club, and swing on the bars. (*Aside.*) Not so much as a sandwich, or a glass of lemonade, nor even a cup of Russian tea.

PERCY.—We fellows are going, Mrs. Thurman, I hope you will excuse us.

BLANCHE.—Oh! certainly, Mr. Graball, remember me kindly to your father; M. Badminton I hope we will see you soon again.

(*Exeunt Percy and Badminton.*)

FLASHEM.— And I think Ma and I must be going; we have an appointment with Mr. Graball for this evening. (*Aside.*) I'm sure old Grab has the whip hand of it, and he's just the very husband for Ma.

(*Exeunt T. Rushington Flashem, and Mrs. Flashem.*)

MRS. VAN HUCKSTER.—I'm awfully vexed, Mrs, Thurman, but we, too, must depart.

VAN HUCKSTER.—Yes, really I'm awfully sorry, but won't you accompany us Lord Flushington ?

LORD FLUSHINGTON.—Oh! so pleased, I'm sure. (*Aside to De la Comare.*) It's getting kind of lonesome, and I always get the shivers, when there's not plenty of people around.

DE LA COMARE, *aside to Flushington.*—Pshaw! you've no nerve, you're not fit to be a lord. (*Aloud.*) Permit me to accompany you also, my dear Mrs. Van Huckster.

(*Exeunt Van Huckster, Mrs. Van Huckster, Lord Flushington and Count de la Comare.*)

ACRITONIA.—I'm sure I'd like to stay, and have a quiet chat, but an unavoidable engagement with the dentist, you know.

TATTLETON, *aside.*—Dentist! why, she hasn't a tooth of her own in her head. (*Aloud.*) And will you permit me the great pleasure of escorting you up the Avenue to Doctor Clip's.

ACRITONIA.—Ah! so delighted, I'm sure. (*Aside.*) I can see that Thurman wants to be alone with his wife. How silly these young people are.

(*Exeunt Tattleton and Acritonia.*)

SCENE XIII.

THURMAN and BLANCHE.

THURMAN.—If you only knew how much I have to say to you, Blanche, you would not avoid me so. If you only knew how full my heart is of tenderness and remorse, aye of remorse, for I know now that what your mother said, what perhaps under the influence of affection for her, you confirmed was false, and that it was not a willing consent which made you my wife.

BLANCHE.—And why should you feel remorse, Mr. Thurman ? It seems an ordinary thing in the society in which we live to disregard the delicacy of young girls, to trample on their pride, and their aspirations.

THURMAN.—Disregard your delicacy, trample on your pride. Ah ! can you not see that I adore you, that there is nothing I would not do to please you, to win one kind, one gentle word from you.

BLANCHE.—And am I ever harsh or impolite when we meet, Mr. Thurman ?

THURMAN.—When we meet, a dozen times since we have been married, and then under the eyes of that crowd of gaping, vulgar, hypocrites. I know I should not have married you without a fuller, truer explanation, but I was mad, mad with infatuation and adoration. Surely a woman can forgive that.

BLANCHE.—A woman can forgive many things, Mr. Thurman; but there is one action that is beyond all pardon, it is that which irrevocably disposes of her whole life, and makes of her present a horror, and of her future a despair.

THURMAN.—A horror! and am I then so detestable, so abhorrent to you. And yet, and yet, I have thought that I saw in your eyes some of the same noble pride I feel in my own heart. I have heard words fall from your lips that have found echos in the depths of my soul, and now, now you are an angel in my eyes. Surely, God could not have made us to be strangers to each other.

BLANCHE.—Let me pass, sir, I— I can listen to no more. Let me pass.

THURMAN.—Never! never! not like that, without a word, without a promise.

BLANCHE.—And would you make an unmanly use of your strength Sir? Let me pass, for I— I hate you.

(*Curtain.*)

ACT III.

(Conservatory and parlor at Mrs. Ketchum's, brilliantly lighted.)

(Enter Tattleton and Flashem, in evening dress.)

SCENE I.

TATTLETON and FLASHEM.

TATTLETON.—I must say Mrs. Ketchum has fitted up her house very magnificently since her daughter's marriage, and her ball to-night is really brilliant.

FLASHEM.—Yes, she must make Thurman pan out a deal of hard cash for the privilege of being the beauty's husband.

TATTLETON.—Yet, they say that was a position you once coveted.

FLASHEM.—Never, I never wanted to marry anyone in my life.

TATTLETON.—But people used to think your attentions to Miss Blanche Ketchum were serious.

FLASHEM.—Serious; I should think they were. Why, when I wanted to water stock, or rope some rich young dudes into a bogus combine, don't you suppose such a paragraph as this in Low Down Antics, was a serious aid to me. The assiduities and compromising attentions of the brilliant, but erratic Chicagoan, T. Rushington Flashem to the reigning beauty, Miss Blanche Ketchum, have caused much gossip, and some malicious and curious reports, which we are, however, reluctant to believe, but which we will confess were very excusable considering the reputation for enterprise, and daring of the young Chicagoan. Don't you suppose such a paragraph as that was sufficient to establish my reputation in the most select circles in the city?

TATTLETON.—But I should have imagined that if it added to your reputation, it might have diminished the lady's.

FLASHEM.—Nonsense, a little scandal helps a woman along in society wonderfully.

TATTLETON.—According to old fashioned notions, after the appearance of such a praragraph, you would have been compelled to shoot the writer, or marry the lady, or both.

FLASHEM.—Shoot a writer in Low Down Antics, stab my benefactor to the heart, nonsense! Besides, we don't marry much in Chicago, we prefer to get divorced.

(*Enter Badminton and Percy Graball.*)

―――

SCENE II.

BADMINTON, PERCY, TATTLETON and FLASHEM.

BADMINTON.—I say, they're fixing up an awful fine feed out there.

PERCY.—Mrs. Ketchum beats everything for jolly balls. Why, I just saw tons of salad, and mountains of champagne out there.

BADMINTON.—And the waiter told me some of it was Pommery extra sec.

TATTLETON.—No wonder; it doesn't cost her anything since her son-in-law pays the bills.

FLASHEM.—And it's a good advertisement besides.

PERCY.—But, I say, Flashem, what's come over Pa, he looked as if he could have danced to-night. Has your Ma been courting him ? I think he's struck with her.

FLASHEM.—Courting him ! never in the world. (*Aside.*) I hope she isn't going too fast, or the old fellow 'ill think he can have everything his own way.

PERCY.—Well, anyway, Pa was awful frisky, and paid some of my poker debts. Well! if it wasn't your Ma, it must have been the fall in wheat then. But come Jack, let us be going.

(*Badminton and Percy go up towards door ; when near it they run against Mrs. Ketchum, who is just entering.*)

MRS. KETCHUM.—If you see your father out there Mr. Graball, will you tell him I would like to speak to him.

PERCY.—All right Mrs. Ketchum, if I lay hands on the governor, I'll haul him to.

BADMINTON, *to Percy.*—Come along! be quick, I hear the corks popping already. If we aint quick, all the champagne 'ill be swashed down by those greedy fellows out there.

(*Exeunt Percy and Badminton*)

SCENE III.

Mrs. KETCHUM, TATTLETON and FLASHEM.

TATTLETON (*aside*, to Flashem.)—Wants to see old Graball ; I wonder if it's another match trust.

FLASHEM (*aside*, to Tattleton.)—I guess not ; people are generally better off before they've seen old Grab than they are afterwards.

Mrs. KETCHUM, *perceiving them.*—Ah! gentlemen, you are not enjoying my ball, then?

FLASHEM. —Oh! yes, we are ; but we came here to discuss stocks. You know that's what a Wall Street man goes to a ball for, to meet some chap he knows and talk stocks with him in a quiet corner.

TATTLETON.—I assure you, Mrs. Ketchum, we are intensely enjoying your charming hospitality. Only a cultivated taste like yours could arrange such exquisite entertainments.

Mrs. KETCHUM.—You are one of the few men remaining in New York who still know how to turn such graceful compliments. You have real, old-time manners, Mr. Tattleton.

(*Enter Van Huckster.*)

SCENE IV.

Mrs. KETCHUM, VAN HUCKSTER, TATTLETON, and FLASHEM.

VAN HUCKSTER.—Oh! Mrs. Ketchum, Ma wants to know if Lord Flushington has come yet. I've been looking everywhere for him.

Mrs. Ketchum.—I don't know, I havn't seen him, but he ought to have been here an hour ago.

Flashem.—Maybe its only English manners, you know they always like to come late, in order to show how much more important they consider themselves than the people whose hospitality they accept.

Van Huckster.—Oh! if it's English manners I'm sure it's correct, and good form.

(*Enter Mrs. Hunter and Ethel.*)

SCENE V.

Mrs. KETCHUM, Mrs. HUNTER, ETHEL, VAN HUCKSTER, TATTLETON, and FLASHEM.

Mrs. Hunter.—Oh! I heard Mr. Van Huckster say he was coming here to ask you about Lord Flushington, so Ethel and I came to inquire about him, as the dear child does enjoy his lordship's company so.

Mrs. Ketchum.—Indeed, I should think he was rather serious company for a young lady. He talks so little; but he will be sure to be here in a few minutes, he never misses one of my entertainments. My house and Mrs. Westmoreland Landonum's are about the only ones he constantly visits.

Mrs. Hunter.—Oh! your house is always so attractive (*aside*); nasty, stuck-up thing; but she hasn't another daughter to marry him to, anyway, so my Ethel's safe.

(*Mrs. Hunter, Mrs. Ketchum and Van Huckster, talk on the left, while Ethel crosses towards Tattleton and Flashem right.*)

ETHEL.—Oh! Mr. Flashem, have you ever traveled in Italy?

FLASHEM.—Never in my life. Slow country, behind hand in speculation. Have no time to study old pictures and cathedrals. Leave that to Ma. Besides, I spent all last summer studying the Eiffel tower, biggest thing in Europe. Why, in six months it paid all the original cost, and brought in twenty per cent. besides. That's an artistic monument worth talking about.

ETHEL.—Oh! but you have visited Italy, I know, Mr. Tattleton.

TATTLETON.—Oh! yes, I spent years there studying the language and literature.

ETHEL.—But did you ever travel in the Appenines?

TATTLETON.—Oh! yes, I took a pedestrian tour there years ago, studying the geological strata which are really most exciting.

ETHEL.—But did you visit many castles there?

TATTLETON.—Why, yes, no end of them.

ETHEL, *taking photograph from her pocket.*—Did you ever see that one?

TATTLETON.—Why, yes, that's the castle of St. Angelo.

ETHEL.—Oh! what a lovely name, how sweet it does sound. Did you know the family who lived there, Mr. Tattleton?

TATTLETON.—Know the family; why it's a prison, Miss Ethel.

ETHEL.—A prison, then there's no aristocratic family in it at all.

TATTLETON.—I don't know, Miss Ethel, sometimes the aristocracy get into queer places.

ETHEL, *aside.*—The horrid mean fellow, if he's deceived me, and he hasn't any castle after all, I shan't go one step with him.

(Ethel goes up towards door.)

MRS. HUNTER.—Ethel, Ethel, where are you going?

ETHEL.—I—— I—— Ma, why, I'm going to look for Lord Flushington.

MRS. HUNTER, *sweetly.*—All right, my dear, go and enjoy yourself, and don't mind me.

(Exit Ethel.)

———

SCENE V.

MRS. KETCHUM, MRS. HUNTER, VAN HUCKSTER, TATTLETON and FLASHEM.

TATTLETON, *to Flashem.*—Do you know what that girl was asking me so much about Italy for?

FLASHEM.—You may take me for anything but a fool. Why, because of that curly-headed ape de la Comare, of course.

TATTLETON.—Why, do you know, I asked Jack Braggart, who professes to know everything, if he could tell me anything about de la Comare. He laughed, and said it was a great tale, and that he would tell me all about it when he had time. I have half a mind to hunt him up this evening, and see what I can learn about it.

(Enter Mrs. Flashem.)

SCENE VI.

Mrs. KETCHUM, Mrs. FLASHEM, Mrs. HUNTER, VAN HUCKSTER, FLASHEM and TATTLETON.

Mrs. Flashem.—Do you know Mr. Graball is out there looking everywhere for you, Mrs. Ketchum?

Mrs. Ketchum.—Indeed, in that case he will certainly find his way here. (*Aside.*) I must not appear too anxious, for then if he really has the upper hand, he will make too hard terms.

Mrs. Flashem, *aside to Flashem.*—I know old Graball wants to propose, shall I let him do it?

Flashem.—No, don't you be too quick about it, don't you gush too much, till I find out whether he's up or down on wheat.

(*Enter Mrs. Van Huckster and Mrs. Acritonia.*)

SCENE VII.

Mrs. KETCHUM, Mrs. HUNTER, Mrs. FLASHEM, Mrs. VAN HUCKSTER, Miss ACRITONIA, VAN HUCKSTER, TATTLETON and FLASHEM.

Mrs. Van Huckster.—Mrs. Ketchum, I've been looking for Lord Flushington everywhere; it's so lonesome out there, there's no one but Americans. (*Aside to Mrs. Ketchum.*) I don't mean you, my dear Mrs. Ketchum, you have a truly English culture, but those restless Western people have no repose of manner.

Flashem.—I tell you what, Mrs. Van Huckster, your English aristocracy is all very well, but in this age when brains and money rule the world, we Americans can give 'em points, and beat 'em every time.

Mrs. Van Huckster, *aside.*—These horrid Chicago people are so noisy and restless, they have no British self-restraint. (*Aloud.*) There are still some distinguished, some princely families, Mr. Flashem, who would be entirely insensible to the influence of money.

Flashem.— I've no doubt that there are plenty of European princes who would stand out against a million or so of dowry, but plague me, if there's a single one of them who wouldn't knock under at ten millions.

Tattleton.—But, Flashem, you don't mean to say, royal princes, why there are some courts in Europe where you can't get in without sixteen quarterings.

Flashem.—When Pa was in the pork trade, he did a deal more quartering than that.

Tattleton. — Anyway they wouln't let you in the Austrian Court, unless you proved sixteen noble ancestors.

Flashem.—Oh ! yes, they would, and by the front door, too. Why, I'd dump down a couple of hundred thousand dollars, and start a newspaper praising up the administration ; I'd edit it myself, then they'd send me as Ambassador to Vienna right off. If the Emperor still proved kind of uppish, and didn't invite me to the family breakfast, why, I'd throw in a million or so of florins and found an orphan asylum, and then if he still put on airs, and didn't come down, I'd marry an Archduchess, or two, I'm sure there are still plenty of old ladies, even in Imperial families, who would be glad to be compromised by a smart young fellow like me.

Mrs. Hunter.—You're the first American I ever saw, Mr. Flashem, who objected to titles.

Flashem.—Object to titles, not a bit of it. On the contrary, I think we've worshipped 'em long enough at a distance, it's about time we introduced 'em here as an economical method of rewarding party services. How much better it would be if all the greedy claimants after a presidential canvass, could be rewarded by being dubbed dukes, instead of shovelling money out of the Treasury to satisfy 'em. And then in place of taking into the administration the fellow who'd carted in the most boodle, when he wasn't fit for it, why they might make him a prince right off. I'm sure that 'ed tickle his wife to death, and do less harm to the country besides. Oh! I don't stop over mere formalities, they're all trash.

Mrs. Van Huckster, *aside to Miss Acritonia.*—Trash! what a low American expression; why couldn't he use the English equivalent, and say rot.

Acritonia.—Do you think that is an improvment, Mrs. Van Huckster, I find it rather startling.

Mrs. Van Huckster.—Oh! it has a real distinction, it's English, you know.

Mrs. Flashem.—Isn't Tommy smart? he gets the better of 'em every time.

Van Huckster.—But you won't deny, Flashem, that in social forms the English excel.

Flashem.—But there's one thing in your English imported fashions, I don't like, it's the way you have of drawing up invitations in New York, now. A chap can never be sure whether they mean to invite or insult him.

Why, an invitation I received last week ran somewhat in this fashion : " Mrs. Westmorland Lundonum summons Mr. Flashem to a musicale at her house, Thursday the 25th. He will be permitted to remain twenty-five minutes."

Van Huckster.—But that's the correct English style.

Flashem.—I should say it was no style at all. Why, it gives a man a cold shiver down his back bone, for he doesn't know if they mayn't end with a threat to take his life, and he's uncertain whether he has received an invitation to somebody else's wedding or his own funeral.

Van Huckster.—But one must expect such formalities from people of position.

Flashem.—I tell you one thing, Van Huckster, we Americans have a deal of faults, but sooner or later we get sick of shams, and people who have to be insolent in order to be important will be found out some day.

Mrs. Van Huckster, *to Miss Acritonia.*—The miserable, low Western man; he doesn't understand British self-restraint.

Mrs. Ketchum.—You, Chicago people, have become very decided in your opinions since you have got the exhibition away from us.

Flashem.—But you went about it in such a stupid way. You kept talking about it's being to the advantage of the whole country to have the show in New York, as if anybody cared for that. But we Chicago boys were much smarter; we sent on a crowd of fellows to Washington with a lot of money, and they bought up everything right, and left and carried through the bill with a rush.

TATTLETON.—I dare say you Chicagoans bought up everything there was buyable in Washington.

FLASHEM.—Oh! no, there isn't enough money in Chicago, nor anywhere else to do that.

(*Enter Jeremiah Graball escorting Blanche.*)

SCENE VIII.

MRS. KETCHUM, MRS. HUNTER, MRS. VAN HUCK-STER, MRS. FLASHEM, ACRITONIA, BLANCHE, JEREMIAH GRABALL, FLASHEM, VAN HUCK-STER and TATTLETON.

FLASHEM, *to Tattleton.*—Just look at old Grab; he's radiant as a new moon. It's all up with Thurman. I'd bet my last dollar on it.

J. GRABALL.—My son told me you were anxious to see me, so you may suppose I hastened to obey orders, and brought Mrs. Thurman with me, too. (*Aside.*) She can't beg much out of me before witnesses.

MRS. KETCHUM —Your son exaggerated if he said I was anxious, but, of course, I'm always delighted to see you, Mr. Graball. (*Aside.*) It won't do to show much feeling, we must keep these low people at a distance.

MRS. VAN HUCKSTER.—Oh! you look awfully lovely, and so gay, Mrs. Thurman. (*Aside.*) Nasty presumptuous thing to refuse my Blackstone.

BLANCHE.—It is very kind of you to say so, but I feel a little weary.

(*Enter Ethel.*)

SCENE IX.

Mrs. KETCHUM, Mrs. HUNTER, Mrs. VAN HUCK-
STER, Mrs. FLASHEM, Miss ACRITONIA, ETHEL,
BLANCHE, JEREMIAH GRABALL, FLASHEM,
VAN HUCKSTER and TATTLETON.

Ethel.—Oh! I say, Ma, I've found Lord Flushington.
(*Aside.*)   Where can Count de la Comare be?

Mrs. Van Huckster.—Oh! let us go, and see what is
the matter with him, I'm sure his Lordship's sick and
suffering.

Mrs. Hunter.—Oh! let us go and see the poor, dear
man.   It quite melts my heart. (*Aside*) As if I were
going to let her have him all to herself.

Ethel.—Oh! I'll go with you, Ma, I do so like to talk
to Lord Flushington. (*Aside.*)   May be I can find de la
Comare; I've been showing the photograph to everyone,
and they all say it is Fra Angelico.   I don't know what
to make of it.   The Count's too lovely for anything, but
I shan't venture unless I can find out about the castle.

(*Exeunt Mrs. Van Huckster, Mrs. Hunter and Ethel.*)

Van Huckster.—I think I'll go too, since Flushington's there.

(*Exit Van Huckster.   Enter Badminton.*)

———

SCENE X.

Mrs. KETCHUM, Mrs. FLASHEM, Miss ACRITONIA,
BLANCHE, JEREMIAH GRABALL, BADMINTON
and TATTLETON.

Badminton, *to Tattleton and Flashem.*—I say boys, the
feed's begun. If you ain't quick you won't get anything

them fellows are swiggering down the champagne by quarts.

TATTLETON.—Yes, I think we'd better go ; it's getting awful dull here ; besides, I want to see Braggart about that Italian.

FLASHEM.—I think I'll remain here awhile yet. (*Aside*) To watch Ma, and see she doesn't compromise herself with old Grab, before I find out how he stands in the market.

TATTLETON.—Miss Acritonia, will you permit me the pleasure of conducting you to the supper-room?

ACRITONIA.—Oh ! certainly; so pleased, Mr. Tattleton.

MRS. FLASHEM, *to Miss Acritonia.*—You'd better not go too far, Miss Acritonia ; I saw Mr. Pogwoggon this morning, and he's going to marry Mrs. Litherford Jumbleton's sixteen-year-old daughter.

ACRITONIA.—Ah ! I think I'll remain here, Mr. Tattleton ; (*aside*) maybe that spiteful woman's deceiving me. (*Aloud.*) After all, I think I'll go ; but no, thanks, I wont take your arm it's too hot.

(*Exeunt Miss Acritonia and Tattleton.*)

———

SCENE X.

FLASHEM, MRS. FLASHEM, BLANCHE, J. GRABALL, and MRS. KETCHUM.

(*Mrs. Ketchum and Graball left, and the others, right.*)

FLASHEM.—I'll keep my eye on Grab and the old woman, and see what's up.

Mrs. Flashem.—I don't bear malice against you, Mrs. Thurman, if you did get the best catch of the season. I'm able to take care of myself, and fortune always favors the persevering, so you won't mind if I tell you you're looking uncommon poorly to-night.

Blanche.—I thank you for your sympathy, Mrs. Flashem; but I assure you I'm feeling exceedingly well, and very cheerful. (*Aside.*) Oh! if I could only get away from this false, miserable life; it's killing me.

Mrs. Flashem.—Then, although its very stylish for married women to go round by themselves, but since its only six weeks since your wedding, some spiteful people were wondering why Mr. Thurman didn't accompany you here. Is he coming, anyway?

Blanche.—I don't know; I—I havn't seen him to-day.

Mrs. Flashem, *aside*.—The silly chit of a girl; such a stunning fine-looking fellow, too.

Mrs. Ketchum, *to J. Graball.*—You may think it strange that I should reproach you after what has occurred, but you know it was my most ardent wish to marry my Blanche to your dear boy; but what would you have? In this world mothers propose but daughters dispose, and the dear child's affection for Mr. Thurman was so irresistable and overwhelming that I was obliged to consent.

Graball.—Oh! don't you mention it, Mrs. Ketchum, it's all forgotten. (*Aside.*) I'll squeeze the life's blood out of 'em, and see how they like that.

Mrs. Ketchum.—I assure you she would'nt listen to my most impassioned protestations; my pleadings, my supplications in favor of your Percy. I tried every-

thing ; I even begged her to have some consideration
for my poor health, but the romantic child would say
nothing but I love Mr. Thurman ; I would die rather
than wed another. What could a tender mother do?

GRABALL.—Oh! I don't doubt that you exerted all
your powers, Mrs. Ketchum. (*Aside.*) As if I didn't
know how she checkmated me.

MRS. KETCHUM.—Then why should you endeavor to
avenge yourself, check all Mr. Thurman's enterprises ;
entangle him into impossible positions ; form combina-
tions against him ; rouse up all trusts in an endeavor
to ruin him ; to impoverish, to beggar, to bankrupt us
all? Oh ! it's unkind, it is unworthy. Mr. Graball, do
you wish to break my heart, and make the whole work
of my life useless?

GRABALL.—It's all Thurman's own fault, Mrs. Ketchum ; what right has he to introduce philosophy into the
stock market ; to talk about basing speculations on a
knowledge of social evolution, international politics,
climatic influences, the growth of crops, and such
things? Why, if it was necessary to understand any
one of them, in order to succeed Wall Street 'ed be
depopulated to-morrow. Not a man 'ed be left in it;
(*raising his voice*,) I'll tell you what's real business
genius, Mrs. Ketchum. It's to make a lot of fellows
sell a lot of stuff they haven't got, and can't get, and
then put on the screws, and squeeze the last penny out
of 'em. Oh! its astonishing the fortunes you can make
out of nothing, in America ; nothing but brains and
bluffing! Yes, that's what I call brains.

(*Enter Thurman, a little before the conclusion of
Graball's speech.*)

SCENE XI.

FLASHEM, Mrs. FLASHEM, BLANCHE, Mrs. KETCHUM, THURMAN, and J. GRABALL.

THURMAN.—Your doctrines, Mr. Graball, show a thorough appreciation of all the sagacity which may spring from the brain, unembarrassed by any of the instincts which arise from the heart.

GRABALL.—Heart! bosh! That's what the people on the losing side always plead. When you were at the top of the heap, you didn't talk such rubbish. But now you expect to move my feelings, to melt my compassion, so that I may give you more time to pay me what I've fairly gained ; what belongs to me.

THURMAN.—Your feelings, your compassion ; that would be adopting your doctrines, and basing my calculations on what does not exist. But you may put your mind perfectly at ease, everything I owe you will be paid, promptly, and in full.

GRABALL, *aside.*—Promptly, and in full. He must have something I knew nothing of laid away.

FLASHEM, *aside, to Mrs. Flashem.*—You can go it now, Ma ; Grab's got the upper hand, and when you catch him, nail him fast.

MRS FLASHEM.—Oh, trust me for that, Tommy. (*Aside.*) The horrid old monster ; what a dose he'll be.

MRS. KETCHUM, (*aside*).—Great heavens, could he have lost all his money? I didn't dream it was as bad as that. How will a divorce look after six week's marriage?

THURMAN, *aside, looking at Blanche.*—If she but had a little sympathy, a little pity for me, I would not mind the rest.

BLANCHE, *aside.*—He looks so pale, so careworn; I wonder if I was wrong, if I was cruel?

MRS. FLASHEM.—I think we're intruding here, in this family party; we'd better go to the drawing-room.

J. GRABALL.—Yes, we'd better go; I hope you bear no malice against me, Mrs. Ketchum, nor you, either, Thurman, it was a fair fight.

MRS. KETCHUM.—Not at all, Mr. Graball; there's no situation so bad that there's not a way out of it. (*Aside.*) Maybe sometime I'd be glad to marry Blanche even to that miserable little fool of a Percy.

FLASHEM, (*to Mrs. Flashem.*)—There, Ma, make advances to old Grab, or he'll escape us.

MRS. FLASHEM.—Oh! Mr. Graball, will you give me your arm? I have something so interesting to tell you.

J. GRABALL.—Delighted, Mrs. Flashem. (*Aside.*) She's stunning stylish; I think I'll have to do the marrying myself.

(*Exeunt Mrs. Flashem, Flashem, and J. Graball.*)

SCENE XII.

BLANCHE, MRS. KETCHUM, and THURMAN.

MRS. KETCHUM.—I am very sorry indeed for your misfortune, Mr. Thurman, but under the circumstances, I am sure you will agree with me that a mother's roof is the only proper place to shelter my daughter in her afflictions.

THURMAN.—Ah! Blanche, if you leave me now, I know, I feel, it will be irrevocably, and forever. But to you I will attribute no sordid motives; I know that all my wealth could not win me your love; but perhaps my misfortunes may give me a right to your compassion.

BLANCHE.—I—I! believe me, I am sorry for you. Only tell me if there is anything I can do, I —

MRS. KETCHUM.—Don't excite yourself, Blanche, my child, or delicate as you are, you're liable to get sick.

THURMAN.—But, Blanche, my dear, little Blanche, if you would but say one kind, one friendly word to me, I would have courage for anything.

MRS. KETCHUM.—Don't you see how you are agitating the poor child; it is cruel, it is ungentlemanly. Just leave her to me, to-night, to soothe and console her and to-morrow you may have any explanation you like. (*Aside.*) I'll know the extent of the disaster then, and what course a conscientious mother should take.

THURMAN.—But can you not see, do you not feel that if we part now it will be forever! Is there no instinct in your heart that bids you say one kind, one gentle word?

MRS. KETCHUM.—Really, I thought you were incapable of such conduct, Mr. Thurman. Having exhausted all reasoning and appeals, my duty as a mother compels me to positively request you to leave here, excited as you are.

THURMAN.—I understand, madame, and I will obey.

(*Exit Thurman.*)

SCENE XIII.

BLANCHE and Mrs. KETCHUM.

Blanche starts forward, as if to follow Thurman; Mrs. Ketchum restrains her.

Mrs. Ketchum.—Would you leave your poor mother, desolate and impoverished, as she is?

Blanche.—I—oh! my heart is breaking.

(*Throws herself in her mother's arms, sobbing hysterically.*)

(*Curtain.*)

ACT IV.

Same as Act III.

(Enter Van Huckster and Mrs. Van Huckster.)

SCENE I.

VAN HUCKSTER and MRS. VAN HUCKSTER.

VAN HUCKSTER.—But isn't this rather sudden, Ma, your engagement to Lord Flushington?

MRS. VAN HUCKSTER.—Sudden, why I've been expecting it for weeks; and then he has a beautiful sister, Blackstone, who I am sure would just suit your aristocratic tastes.

VAN HUCKSTER.—But wouldn't that be rather a queer kind of proceeding, Ma, if you were to marry the brother, wouldn't it be kind of bigamous, or trigamous, or something?

MRS. VAN HUCKSTER.—Why, then he has a cousin, a lovely cousin, Lady Gwendolen Frangandon.

VAN HUCKSTER.—I'm sure her name's very attractive; I'm quite willing, Ma, on two conditions: that she doesn't wear a silver necklace, nor a round cap with lavender ribbons on it.

MRS. VAN HUCKSTER.—I'm awfully shocked; Blackstone, how can you—the daughter of an English nobleman with a silver necklace—who ever saw such a thing?

Van Huckster.—Oh, I did, Ma, at a ball in Belgravia. Danced with a daughter of Sir Francis Ironspyke, and she wore a flame-colored gauze, and a silver necklace with a dozen full-size, silver mackerel dangling from it.

Mrs. Van Huckster.—Silver mackerel, and flame-colored gauze! What a lovely, English combination.

(Enter Badminton.)

SCENE II.

VAN HUCKSTER, BADMINTON, and MRS. VAN HUCKSTER.

Badminton.—Oh, I say, Van Huckster, there's an awful row out there. A man has come after Lord Flush-ington, and is making a regular circus out in the entry. I don't half like the looks of it.

Mrs. Van Huckster.—After Lord Flushington! Oh' it must be some of his relatives.

Van Huckster.—Yes, Ma, let's go and see them.

(As they are going out, enter Percy Graball, and Flashem.)

SCENE III.

FLASHEM and PERCY GRABALL.

Percy.—It's awful hard lines on Mrs. Ketchum, her son-in-law loosing all his money like that. They say he left the house, half an hour ago, dead-broke. Just six weeks after her daughter had married him, too. Do you know I came near marrying her myself?

Flashem.—Who, Mrs. Ketchum, or her daughter?

Percy.—Oh, the daughter, of course.

Flashem.—Why, the daughter, of course? The mother's much the smartest; but I suppose when Miss Ketchum married another fellow, you were awful cut up about it, you boys are so queer.

Percy.—Oh, no I wasn't, I was very glad, for I think it was awful hard lines of Pa to try and pull me up short like that, and marry me before I'd had my fling. To be sure, he said I might fling all I liked after I was married, but that was no go.

Flashem.—Why not? I should think the arrangement would have suited perfectly.

Percy.—Oh, no it didn't; I was too afraid of Blanche's Ma.

Flashem.--I see you're a pretty sharp fellow after all, for if a man wants a tranquil life after he's married, the woman he should study is not his wife, but his mother-in-law. But I'll tell you a woman who'd make a real, docile mother-in-law to a rich young man, if she could only get him.

Percy.—Who is she? Do tell me, for I know Pa 'ill marry me some time, he has a perfect mania for it.

Flashem.—It's Mrs. Hunter; she'd be so awful glad to get you; she'd be sure to treat you nice.

(*Enter Tattleton.*)

SCENE IV.

TATTLETON, FLASHEM, and PERCY.

Tattleton, *laughing.*—Oh, I have such a funny tale to tell you, only it will take me some time to get through with it.

Percy.—Then I'll go ; my brain can't stand a prolonged strain.

(*Exit Percy.*)

SCENE V.

TATTLETON and FLASHEM.

Flashem.—What's the joke, Tattleton ? It seems to give you a vast amount of amusement.

Tattleton. It's all about that curly-headed Italian barber.

Flashem.—What is he, a brigand.

Tattleton.—The fun of it all is that he isn't an Italian at all, but a New York news-boy ; Jack Braggart has been telling me all about him. He was an assistant to an Italian barber in Bleecker street, and Braggart says he doesn't believe he speaks one word of Italian, but must have got his name from a copy of the opera Crispino e la Comare.

Flashem.—But how in the deuce did he get his Italian accent ?

Tattleton.—Who knows ; he may speak Italian with an English accent. I've a mind to try him. Braggart says that when he recognized him, De la Comare, or Billy Jones—that's his real name—begged him not to expose him, and said if he'd let him have one more spree to-night, he'd clear out to-morrow, and try the dodge somewhere else ; but I don't think there's any place on earth where a foreign nobleman can succeed as well as in New York.

FLASHEM.— But its my opinion that if he does'nt make off mighty soon, he may take that little fool of an Ethel Hunter with him ; she seems so interested in everything Italian lately, even if it comes from Bleecker street.

TATTLETON.—Maybe I'd better try and frighten him off. But, I say, Flashem, do you really think Thurman's dead broke, and Graball's got all his money? Its a shame ; because, in spite of his want of education, Thurman's quite a gentleman, and knows how to give an entertainment.

FLASHEM.—But, do you know, I think old Graball, with all his pluck and go, has a soft place in his upper story.

TATTLETON.—A soft place ; why, I should think he was as hard as flint.

FLASHEM.—But just look at the way he goes to work to get into society ; why, he tries to marry his son to a fashionable beauty in order to get her social connections, as if they wouldn't drop her as soon as she ceased to be useful.

TATTLETON.—But, with his manners and exterior, I don't see any other way he could go to work.

FLASHEM.—Manners and exterior ; bosh! who cares for manners or exterior, when there's as much money as that? If a man has a million or two, they may ask questions, but if he has thirty or forty of 'em, never! Why didn't he go to work, rationally, get the very biggest house he could lay hands on ; buy a stock of pictures, the dearest he could get, and have the prices he paid for them advertised in all the papers, then pay 'em to give long accounts of the frescoing and furnishing ; the wood-carvings he had selected, himself from châteaus, and churches, and the old tapestry he had inherited from some remote ancestor, recently dead ; and then everybody would be curious to see the inside of his house, and glad of an invitation.

TATTLETON.—Yes, it is astonishing how much old tapestry and family relics you New Yorkers have all inherited lately ; and yet, the bric-a-brac shops always keep well supplied. I don't know how they manage it.

FLASHEM.—Oh! I suppose they have formed a joint trust, and change the same ancestors, and the same relics around among 'em? But then, the proper thing to do would be to give a monster entertainment, and have it advertised in all the papers that it would cost $200,000, and would be the most expensive ever seen in New York. Then do something novel ; turn the back yard into a conservatory, or hire the block opposite, and throw bridges across the street. And then have it noised about that every lady who came would receive a bouquet of orchids costing a hundred dollars, and that every gentleman would get a new patent opera hat, with a concealed receptacle for coffee beans. He might get them both wholesale cheap, and the thing would be done ; and I'll wager the whole 1,500 would turn in at the entertainment.

(Excited noise of screams and tramping.)

TATTLETON.—Oh! I'm sure something's up; I must go and see.

(*Exit Tattleton.*)

————

SCENE VI.

FLASHEM.—I wonder how much money old Grab's made in that wheat deal. He must have got pretty near all Dan Thurman had, and I wonder exactly how much that was. It must have been a jolly fine pile, somewhere up in the twenties. A man who could do that so neatly in a few weeks must have lots of points to give. I'm beginning to be anxious about Ma; she may spoil everything by gushing too much.

(*Enter Mrs. Flashem.*)

————

SCENE VII.

FLASHEM and MRS. FLASHEM.

MRS. FLASHEM.—I say, Tommy, it's done. I got old Grab in a corner where he could'nt escape, and nailed him on the spot.

FLASHEM.—Ma, I'm proud of you, but did you fix a date for the wedding?

MRS. FLASHEM.—No, I didn't think of that; besides, we hadn't time, for the whole thing only took five minutes. Old Grab said: let us form a joint stock company.

FLASHEM.—Well, what did you say?

MRS. FLASHEM.—I said, how much will you put in? Then he said: all I've got. Then I said, you couldn't do better ; so we shook hands on it, and he wanted to kiss me, but I objected, for I dont like to be kissed by a bald-headed man. It's a weakness I have. Besides, if I get sick of the old fellow, after I've been married a little while, I'll make him pan me out a fine income, and then I'll go and live in Paris.

FLASHEM.—Oh, no you don't, Ma, for who'd give me points then? We couldn't telegraph 'em back and forth; besides if you left the field, half my strength'd be gone.

MRS. FLASHEM.—All right, Tommy, I'll try and put up with the old codger for a while ; but look here, you won't turn on us both and cheat us, will you?

FLASHEM.—Could you think such a thing of me, Ma? (*Aside.*) I'll skin the old fellow every time. Just give me eighteen months and I'll get the last cent he has. Then I'll send Ma to live in Paris, and she'll be completely happy.

(*Noise and confusion outside ; and enter Mrs. Van Huckster, hysterical and half fainting, supported by Van Huckster and Count de la Comare.*)

SCENE VIII.

FLASHEM, MRS. FLASHEM, MRS. KETCHUM, MRS. HUNTER, BLANCHE, ETHEL, ACRITONIA, TATTLETON, BADMINTON, JEREMIAH GRAB-ALL, and PERCY.

MRS. VAN HUCKSTER.—Oh, Blackstone, Blackstone ! Let us go away from this horrid place; let us go and live in London.

TATTLETON.—Here, Mrs. Van Huckster, here are some salts.

MRS. VAN HUCKSTER, *faintly*.—Are they English salts?

TATTLETON.—Yes, the genuine article with Her Majesty's portrait on every bottle.

MRS. VAN HUCKSTER.—Oh, how sweet it smells! how the balmy English odor revives me.

BADMINTON.—But may be, Mrs. Van Huckster, there may be some mistake about it.

PERCY.—Yes, may be they mistook Lord Flushington for some other fellow.

J. GRABALL.—No, it was all stiff and straight, and he had it down in black and white. This fellow who has been humbugging us into the belief he was a lord is a common bank-burglar. There's no doubt of it. His real name is Jim Wilkins, and he robbed a bank in Manchester three months ago, and has been going it on the proceeds ever since. (*Aside.*) And to think of all the Madeira he's drunk up at my house.

MRS. KETCHUM.—I'm afraid there is no hope, Mrs. Van Huckster, but we were all deceived. (*Aside.*) What a fool the woman made of herself.

MRS. HUNTER.—I'm sure I always suspected him. (*Aside.*) And I came so near marrying Ethel to him. I must look around somewhere else.

PERCY.—What are you looking for, Mrs. Hunter? Can I aid you?

MRS. HUNTER, *aside*.—It seems like the voice of providence. (*Aloud.*) You're the very one I wanted to see. Will you bring my Ethel to me. The dear child is so timid in company.

Percy.—Oh, awfully delighted, I'm sure. (*Aside.*) Flashem was right ; she's the very mother-in-law for me—so quiet and subdued. I'll make up to her.

Acritonia, *to Mrs Flashem.*—The idea of an old woman like that fainting.

Mrs. Flashem.—Oh, its the very thing for her, it makes her look nervous, and interesting ; but I should think she'd have killed herself with all the salts she sniffed.

Mrs. Ketchum, *to Blanche.*—If you look so melancholy people will suspect something.

Blanche, *aside.*—God have pity on me ; I know not what I ought to do.

Mrs. Van Huckster.—Yes, thank you, Count de la Comare, the cushions are very nicely arranged. It is a comfort to have some one near me, who can really sympathize with me. (*Aside.*) An Italian count is not an English lord, but he's better than these horrid, noisy Americans.

Comare.—Oh, Madam ! is there no leetle service I could render you.

Mrs. Van Huckster, *languidly.*—No, thanks.

Comare, *aside.*—This affair of poor Wilkins has made me feel awful ticklish, but being a little lighthanded at cards, can't be punished with hard labor ; still, anyway, I'll be off mighty soon. (*Leaning over Ethel's chair.*) My lofe, my beautiful lofe, vil you not flee vid me to-night.

Ethel, *sotto voce.*—There's no use of asking me, Count de la Comare. I'll never go unless I'm sure about the castle. Too many poor, American girls have been cheated out of their castles by Italian counts.

COMARE.—Oh, you are cruel, my beautiful lofe. (*Aside.*) There's no go here ; I'll have to give it up, and try a Philadelphia heiress, no newsboy could beat her.

TATTLETON.—Just look at that barber fellow hanging over the little Hunter ; if I dont expose him soon, he'll carry her off under our very eyes.

FLASHEM.—Oh, she has a sharp eye to the main chance herself. I guess she wont risk anything.

TATTLETON.—I say, De la Comare, all these ladies think they'd love to hear a native speak Italian ; as they've only heard it spoken in American schools, and haven't the least idea of what it is like.

COMARE.—Oh, but you Boston people are so cultivated ; you speak all foreign tongues so beautifully ; ef you were to say something to me, jist to start the conversation, and then I'd answer it.

TATTLETON, *aside.*—Damn the fellows brass ! (*Aloud.*) Of course I speak Italian, count ; we speak all languages in Boston, only we don't care to display our learning before company, and before natives especially. It's bad taste, you know.

COMARE, *aside.*—Doesn't know a word of Italian ; I thought so. (*Hemming and hawing.*) Well, if the ladies desire it—Scelleratini di Bleeckerini, pettini e spazzolini, sapone prestissimo, monellino maladetto, Ecco—vid the Toscan accent, ladies.

TATTLETON, *stunned.*—I wonder if he really does speak Italian.

Chorus of all the women.—Oh, that is lovely, count, lovely.

Mrs. Van Huckster.—Yes, it is awfully nice. It has a really English sound.

Badminton.—Of course it has. Italian is nothing but English with ino, and ina added to it. We all know that.

Comare.—Oh, that's sometimes the case, but its not always so.

Tatlteton.—And yet, if you take the English word barber and turn it into Italian, it makes Barberini.

Comare, *after a pause.*—And den van you torn it bak in Anglish, it mak barbarian.

Flashem, *aside.*—He's an American ; no blarsted foreigner 'ed be smart enough for that.

Comare, *aside.*—I think I'd better be off, while I'm still on top. (*Aloud.*) Ladies, I dink I most excuse meselve, I've a most pressing and unavoidable engagement vid my banker. (*Aside.*) I'll have a parting fling at poker.

Mrs. Van Huckster.—Oh, count, dont go, it will be so awfully lonesome. (*Aside.*) No one but those wretched Americans left.

J. Graball, *aside.*—Banker! I wonder if he really has any money. I'll see to this. What business has a fellow like that to keep any money. I'll get him into some speculation.

Chorus of all the women.—Oh, count! do come and see us to-morrow. Oh, count ! we're so sorry you're going to leave. Oh, count! don't miss my ball. Oh, count!

remember my five o'clock. Oh, count! don't forget my luncheon, *etc., etc.*

Comare.—Oh, indeed, I shall not, ladies ; I shall go to every one of them. (*Aside.*) I'll be off for Philadelphia by the five o'clock train to-morrow morning to look for an heiress.

(*Exit De la Comare.*)

SCENE IX.

BLANCHE, Mrs. KETCHUM, ETHEL, Mrs. HUNTER, Miss ACRITONIA, Mrs. VAN HUCKSTER, Mrs. FLASHEM, FLASHEM, TATTLETON, VAN HUCKSTER, J. GRABALL, PERCY, and BADMINTON.

Flashem, *to Tattleton.*—I tell you, the more I think about that affair of Thurman's, the queerer it seems to me. A smart fellow like that to fall in love, and neglect the stock market for the sake of a woman. Why, he's the last survival of an extinct race, and ought to be put on exhibition. Millions might be made by it, for I'm sure everybody in America would rush to see what such a man could look like.

Tattleton.—But the more I think about it, the more sorry I am that Thurman's lost his money, for that man Graball will never learn how to give a decent dinner.

Mrs. Van Huckster.—I'm sorry, Mrs. Ketchum, but my head aches so awfully, that I must go.

Mrs. Ketchum.—Oh, not so soon, I hope. Come here, Blanche, and help entertain Mrs. Van Huckster.

(*Blanche, who has kept apart, joins the group.*)

Mrs. Ketchum, *to Blanche.*—If you look so gloomy, everybody 'll think you're fretting about that fellow, Thurman. (*To Mrs. Van Huckster.*) I'm sure I was very sorry about that Flushington affair, but any one could have seen the man was not a real English nobleman.

Mrs. Van Huckster, *aside.*—Nasty, malicious thing. (*Aloud.*) By the way, Mrs. Thurman, when you break up, wont you let me know, so that I may engage that lovely English butler of yours. I think he's just too sweet.

Mrs. Flashem.—Why, I don't know how you can want him. I think he's a downright, cheeky chap.

Miss Acritonia.—So you are going to break up, Mrs. Thurman?

Mrs. Hunter.—Oh, I'm really sorry for you, Mrs. Thurman, I assure you. It must be such a disappointment to you, just at the beginning of the season, too. (*Aside.*) Horrid, stuck up thing, its time she was taken down.

Blanche.—I assure you, Mrs. Hunter, the more I see of society, the less disappointment it will be to me to be deprived of its gayeties.

Mrs. Ketchum.—How the child does talk, as if there was any such prospect as that. Mr. Thurman has grossly deceived us, Mrs. Hunter, and we will find it very difficult to forgive him. Whatever his misfortunes may be, there is no reason why my daughter should be deprived of the gayeties suitable to her age and social position.

Mrs. Hunter.—I always thought there was something

suspicious about him.   (*Aside.*)   She had her trouble for her pains any way, and served her right, too ; nasty, artful thing.

Mrs. Van Huckster.—Then he had no distinction about him—no English repose of manner.

Mrs. Flashem.—For my part I think he was a stunning, fine-looking chap, any way, but rather heady.   (*Aside.*) The idea of his marrying that little chit of a girl.

Ethel.—I think he was a real masher, any way.

Mrs. Hunter.—Ethel, you ought to be ashamed to use such vulgar language.

Miss. Acritonia.—But, did you notice what a large foot he had ?

Mrs. Flashem.—We never notice feet in Chicago.

Miss Acritonia.—Oh, my ! I should think you would.

Mrs. Van Huckster.—I was really surprised when I heard you permitted him to marry your daughter, Mrs. Ketchum, for you know he really never had any ancestors.

Tattleton.—Yes, they say he came from a very low family.

J. Graball.—They say he was born in a log cabin with one room in it.

Percy.—And that his father was a squatter.

Badminton.—And his mother a cook.

Van Huckster.—And that he was turned out of the cow-boys for stealing horses.

Mrs. Van Huckster.—And that he cheated a poor English syndicate out of some silver-mines.

Mrs. Hunter.—And that he stole, right and left.

Mrs. Ketchum.—Oh, if I had only known all these frightful things before, I would never have risked my poor Blanche's happiness ; but, luckily, the law can free her from such a dreadful man.

Blanche.—Mamma!

Flashem.—But he's a right, down smart fellow, any way. Why, some one told me that he bought up a whole legislature out West, and got 'em to put the State Capitol in a place where he'd a lot of swamp land that he had taken for a five dollar poker debt, and made millions out of the deal. I tell you, the fellow who can do that is sure to get up again. There's no telling to what heights the country may mount if that kind of thing goes on much longer.

Mrs. Van Huckster, *aside to Van Huckster.*—I think we'd better be leaving ; these horrid Americans are so noisy.

Van Huckster.—Yes, Ma, let us sail for Liverpool next Saturday, and turn our high-bred backs on this land of vulgarity. Good evening, Mrs. Ketchum, good evening.

(*Exeunt Van Huckster and Mrs. Van Huckster.*)

Mrs. Hunter, *aside to Ethel.*—There's no use of staying here any longer, this woman's ruined. (*Aloud.*) Will you conduct my daughter to the carriage, Mr. Graball ; she's so timid.

Percy.—Awfully pleased, I'm sure. (*Aside.*) She's so mild and docile ; she's just the mother-in-law I'd like. I'll propose if I can, going down the stairs.

ETHEL.—Oh, Mr. Graball, you're always so entertaining. (*Aside.*) He's a horrid fool, but Ma says its the only chance I've got.

(*Exeunt Mrs. Hunter, Ethel, and Percy.*)

J. GRABALL, *aside.*—Looks like a match. Guess I'll follow and see it comes off, for that scrumptious little girl is getting on in society, and will succeed that fool of a Blanche, now the place is vacant. I'll just see it comes off; besides there's no use of ceremony with these people now I've got their money. (*Aloud.*) My dear Mrs. Flashem, may I call early to-morrow morning to talk about the happy day.

MRS. FLASHEM.—Yes, Jerry, just as early as ever you like—the sooner the better. (*Aside.*) The horrid old bore ; I don't believe he has a hair on his head.

J. GRABALL.—Good evening. Good evening, all.

(*Exit J. Graball.*)

TATTLETON.—Miss Acritonia, may I have the pleasure of conducting you down?

MISS ACRITONIA.—Oh, certainly, Mr. Tattleton.

BADMINTON, *to Tattleton.*—Oh, I say, don't you gush too much. Didn't you hear the news? Why, Mrs. Dinever has just adopted the orphan daughter of a distant cousin, and made her her heiress.

TATTLETON, *to Badminton.*—Is it possible! (*To Miss Acritonia.*) Now I think of it, I have pressing business with Flashem, so maybe Badminton will take you down.

MRS. FLASHEM, *to Acritonia.*—Don't you let him go, Miss Acritonia, for I know Mr. Pogwoggon is taking heavy suppers of terrapin stew and waffles every night, and may die any time.

Miss Acritonia.—No. If four hours of Wagner didn't kill 'im, he'll survive the terrapin stew and waffles. No, Mrs. Flashem, I've lost all hope. There's no luck in this world for me.

Badminton.—May I have the pleasure, Miss Acritonia. By the way, do you know you were real mean not to invite me to your afternoon teas?

Miss Acritonia.—I shall never forget you again, Mr. Badminton. (*Aside.*) But, besides, he's too young, and he has no money.

Badminton.—Awfully kind of you, Miss Acritonia. (*Aside.*) They say she has real old-fashioned sandwiches at those teas. None of those mean little modern shams, but great solid things as big as your head.

(*Exeunt Miss Acritonia and Badminton.*)

Tattleton.—I don't know how you can tolerate that fellow Badminton, Mrs. Ketchum ; he's so boisterous and then he comes of a very low family, you know.

Mrs. Ketchum.—Yes, I know all his people are low, but they hold high positions at Washington, and may be useful.

Tattleton.—I know it's always well to be politic, Mrs. Ketchum. (*Aside.*) It's getting awful dull here, but maybe it wont do to break with the old woman, she's so full of resources. (*Aloud.*) Good evening, Mrs Ketchum, I'll be around to-morrow morning, if you will permit me. (*Aside.*) Maybe by that time I can see how the ground lies.

Mrs. Ketchum.—Certainly, with pleasure, Mr. Tattleton.

Tattleton.—Good evening, Mrs. Flashem; good evening, Flashem; I'm sure I wish you good evening also, Mrs. Thurman.

(Exit Tattleton.)

Flashem, *aside.*—What fools these fellows all are to turn their backs on Dan. Why, he has such a gift of the gab that he's sure to get to the top of the heap in politics, and then what bills he could rush through Congress for me. I'll go and see him this very evening. (*Aloud.*) I've a pressing affair on hand now, Mrs. Ketchum, and so I must be off, but I'll be around early to-morrow morning to see Mrs. Thurman, and you also.

Mrs. Flashem.—I'm sure I don't bear people any malice for being unfortunate. I hope everything will turn out all right.

(*Flashem and Mrs. Flashem, after parting greetings to Blanche and Mrs. Ketchum, pause near the door.*)

Flashem, *to Mrs. Flashem.*—I have some pressing business on hand, Ma, and mayn't see you till to-morrow afternoon, but you watch old Grab close, and see he doesn't slip through your fingers; and I'll tell you what I'll do if I am successful next year, I'll take you on a trip to Paris. (*Aside.*) I want to study that tower again; its immense.

Mrs. Flashem.—Oh, Tom, you're too sweet for anything. I just love Paris.

Flashem.—I know you do, Ma. You wouldn't be an American woman if you didn't. (*Aside.*) They should have built that tower underground, and then they might have struck a mine on the way that would have paid the costs, and the rest would have been clear profit.

(*Exeunt Flashem and Mrs. Flashem.*)

SCENE X.

Mrs. KETCHUM and BLANCHE.

Mrs. Ketchum.—Why, you're more like you were crazy than anything I ever saw. I could hardly hold you. Did you want to make an exhibition of us before all those people.

Blanche.—Ah! he treated me cruelly, but he at least was in earnest, and when I heard those contemptible people dare to abuse him in my presence, my whole soul revolted. I despised myself for remaining silent. I felt as base, and mean as they.

Mrs. Ketchum.—You wouldn't have been insane enough to add to the scandal by answering them.

Blanche.—I know he did wrong to force me to marry him, but maybe a man's ideas of right and wrong are different from mine, and then—then I think he loved me, and now that he is ruined, desolate, and deserted— I cannot be harsh to him, I—I forgive him, and I am going to tell him so.

(*Goes up towards door.*)

Mrs. Ketchum.—But you obstinate, insane child, listen to me. I know you think he cornered the Wall street market, and risked millions of dollars in order to win you. You, in your childish vanity imagine that he staked his whole fortune for the privilege of becoming the husband of a little chit of a girl like you. But not a word of that is true.

BLANCHE.—Not true! what do you mean, Mamma, what do you mean?

MRS. KETCHUM.—You think it was Thurman cornered the market, and made me lose nearly all the money I had in order to force you to marry him. But you can give up that sweet illusion. It wasn't Thurman at all; it was old Jeremiah Graball did it.

BLANCHE.—Graball! Oh, my God!

MRS. KETCHUM.—Yes, it was Graball who did it all, and then he came and offered to put up the money for the margins, if you would marry his Percy. I, like the fond and devoted mother, I am, thought of a way to at once save our little property, and ensure your future, and happiness by giving you a husband whom I then thought more suitable, but whom I now see to be most unworthy. If you had not been so foolish I would not have needed to tell you any fibs, but I can say now most conscientiously that that fellow Thurman had nothing at all to do with the match-trust affair.

BLANCHE.—Nothing at all to do with it! and I have been so cruel to him! I have tried so hard to despise him for the sake of my own self-respect.

MRS. KETCHUM.—Yes, despise him, he deserves it, I can assure you—to deceive us so shamefully about his property. Just listen to me, and I'll——

BLANCHE.—Listen to you, never, never again. Can't you see what a wicked thing it was to dispose of your daughter's life and make it impossible for her to give her heart with it? Oh, you have been cruel, unnatural.

You let him beg me for one kind word—one sign of gentle sympathy in his ruin and despair, and, while every womanly instinct of my heart was pleading in his favor, you said not one word to dissolve that false, that wretched memory which closed my lips. Oh, you have made me act a base, an unworthy, an ignoble part. You are my mother, but I will never forgive you.

(*Goes up toward background.*)

Mrs. Ketchum.—Blanche! Blanche! where are you going? Not to that man? Didn't you hear what all those people said of him? You said yourself you did not love him ; you told me so.

Blanche.—Did I say that? Maybe it was not true then. It is a thousand times untrue now.

Mrs. Ketchum.—But you wouldn't desert your mother —your poor, old mother in her disappointment and desolation. Don't you know I might die any day, delicate as I am? Have you no pity?

Blanche.—No, mother, I have no pity for you nor for any one but him, for he alone deserves it.

(*Curtain.*)

ACT V.

(Library in Thurman's house. Bookcases, large square table, centre. Doors r. and l. Thurman seated behind table, facing audience, examining papers.)

SCENE I.

THURMAN.

THURMAN.—Who would have thought that a little delicate creature like that could be so cruel. What a fool a man is to think because a woman's beauty fires his heart, that all noble and generous sentiments must be natural to her. And yet—and yet—bah! I will not think of it any more; it unnerves me. I will live it down—this heartbreak. I will be some use in the world yet.

(Enter Stiffneck, cautiously opening door on the right.)

SCENE II.

THURMAN and STIFFNECK.

STIFFNECK.—Mr. Thurman, sir, I've been wantin' to speak to you for the last 'alf hour.

THURMAN.—Well, what is it, Stiffneck?

STIFFNECK.—Hit's h'only this, sir : h'I was thinkin' h'as h'every man must look h'out for 'imself, maybe h'I'd do wrong not to h'accept Mrs. Van Huckster's h'offers h'as she seems so very h'urgent about h'it.

THURMAN.—So Mrs. Van Huckster has been making you an offer, has she. Wants you to go live with her as butler, I suppose. Well, would you like a reference before you leave?

STIFFNECK.—H'I 'ope you wont be h'offended, sir, but h'I wont trouble you, sir. (*Aside.*) H'a reference from h'a man who's lost 'is money could h'only h'injure h'a poor duffer h'in New York.

THURMAN.—When are your wages due?

STIFFNECK.—H'I can't h'exactly tell, but h'I was paid ten days h'ago, h'and they pays me h'every month.

THURMAN.—Then, I should surmise, after careful arithmetical calculation that they might be due in about three weeks. Well, here are the month's wages.

STIFFNECK.—Thanks, h'awfully ; but considerin' the h'abrupt circumstances h'under which h'I'm h'obliged to leave, don't you think h'a real gentleman like you h'ought to give me somethin' h'extra?

THURMAN.—I don't know about the obligation of the matter, but here's an extra month's wages ; does that satisfy you?

STIFFNECK.—H'I'm sure h'I'm h'awfully h'obliged, sir, but h'I think h'I'd better be h'off, for Mrs. Van Huckster 'as h'already sent seven messenger boys h'after me, h'and h'I'm h'afraid she may h'eat me h'if h'I don't go quick.

THURMAN.—Very well, Stiffneck ; I hope you will get along.

STIFFNECK.—Thanks, h'awfully, h'I'm sure. (*Aside.*) H'anyway h'I get h'away from that vixen Suzette. H'I'm sure 'er bank h'account h'is h'all a sham, h'or she'd let me look h'in the book.

(*Exit Stiffneck.*)

———

SCENE III.

THURMAN.

THURMAN.—Even the servants have found out my ruin. Ah, well ; they are no worse than the others

(*A knock is heard at the door.*)

THURMAN.—Come in.

(*Enter Suzette.*)

———

SCENE IV.

THURMAN and SUZETTE.

SUZETTE.—Shure and I hope you'll excuse me, sor, but I wanted to see you.

THURMAN.—You want to go away also, is it not so ?

SUZETTE.—I'm shure I do hope you'll excuse me, but I'm not as strong as I used to be, and I thought a nice, quiet place with an elderly lady might suit me.

THURMAN.—So you are going to live with Miss Acritonia, perhaps?

Suzette.—Oh, no, sir, she's too young and flighty. I'm going to live with Mrs. Ketchum.

Thurman.—Mrs. Ketchum !

Suzette.—Shure ; and yes, its such a nice quiet place. (*Aside.*) But didn't we help used to have high jinks there ; and the old lady's so smart—she'll always keep afloat.

Thurman.—I suppose you want your wages ; when are they due?

Suzette.—Shure, Sor', and they were due last night.

Thurman, *handing money.*—And they didn't pay you?

Suzette.—But shure, sir, and they did ; but I thought as I'd been so long in the family, you might give me something extra. Then I'm going to live with Mrs. Thurman again.

Thurman.—Ah !

Suzette.—Yes ; for shure and we all know she'll live with her mother now.

Thurman.—You may leave Suzette.

Suzette.—Very well, Sor. (*Aside.*) Any way, I'll get rid of that tantalizing Englishman, for I'm sure all his rich relatives in the ould countree are a sham.

(*Exit Suzette.*)

SCENE V.

THURMAN.

Thurman.—Even the domestics knew she would leave me.

(*A knock is heard at the door and Thurman rises and opens it.*)

(*Enter Flashem.*)

SCENE VI.

THURMAN and FLASHEM.

Thurman.—Ah, is that you, Tom? I did not expect you this evening.

Flashem.—Oh, I thought the sight of a friendly face might do you good. (*Aside.*) I hope that he isn't so dead-broke that it will keep him out of Congress till the elections are over.

Thurman.—You are right, it does do me good to see one honest face.

Flashem.—Now, what did I ever do to you, Dan, that you should insult me like that? In our days, no man's called honest unless he's too plagued a fool to improve his opportunities.

Thurman.—I am sure that it was far from my intentions to insult you when I applied that epithet to you.

Flashem.—I forgive you. We'll say no more about it. Let us talk about your affairs. I'll tell you one thing, Dan, I've been reading over your campaign speeches, and I'm convinced political life's the thing for you. Have you made up your mind about accepting that nomination to Congress? Ah, Congress! that's the place for you ; your talents are lost here.

THURMAN.—I have not made up my mind yet, but whatever I do, I will not remain long in New York.

FLASHEM.—Go West, Dan, go West. I'll tell you the truth, I don't think you're suited to this community, any way. But go to Congress ; that's the thing for you. There's nothing like that to reestablish a fortune quick. But I hope you've got something left over—some little surplus?

THURMAN.—Yes, I have a little; two hundred thousand dollars perhaps.

FLASHEM.—That's right, there's nothing like a little money to begin politics with. But, I say, Dan, when you get the whip hand on Congress, wont you rush through a few bills for me?

THURMAN.—What kind of bills?

FLASHEM.—Oh, I have a dozen or so of railroads out West that are running on mighty rickety rails just now, and the only thing that can boost 'em up would be a good plastering with Congressional cement ; and so you will give me a helping hand, wont you, Dan ?

THURMAN.—If your bills are not contrary to the general interests of the country I'll do all I can. (*Aside.*) So this was the secret of his coming.

FLASHEM.—I wont keep you any longer, Dan, you're looking real tired ; you'd better go to bed, and rest ; and so, good bye, I'll see you again about those railroads. (*Aside.*) I think that's all fixed. Now for old Grab.

(*Exit Flashem.*)

SCENE VII.

THURMAN.

THURMAN.—So his purpose too was selfish. I wonder if there is any generous and noble heart left in this world.

(*The door opens slowly, and enter Blanche—Thurman does not perceive her at first.*)

SCENE VIII.

BLANCHE and THURMAN.

THURMAN.—I see it more and more clearly every day that if a man wishes to be true to himself—to preserve any lofty or generous aspirations, he must live alone.

BLANCHE,—Alone! no not alone, for I——

THURMAN.—Blanche! my little Blanche! (*Catches her in his arms.*) You do not hate me then? You come to me when all the others have deserted me?

BLANCHE.—Oh, I have been harsh, I have been cruel. How you must have despised me when you thought I was like the others, driven away by misfortune.

THURMAN.—Like the others? No, never like the others to me.

BLANCHE.—But they deceived me. I deceived myself; for I know that in the depths of my heart, I did not—I could not believe them. I knew that you who were so proud and so gentle could not be so base.

THURMAN.—Deceived you! What did they tell you, my little Blanche?

BLANCHE.—They told me that you left me the choice between reducing my mother to a hopeless poverty and giving you my hand.

THURMAN.—And you could believe that infamous thing of me—of me who loved you with my whole heart?

BLANCHE.—Alas! it was my mother who told me.

THURMAN.—Ah!

BLANCHE.—But can we not leave this horrible place?

THURMAN.—The place is not horrible; it is the insincere and selfish people who make it appear so. But we will go away—far away to begin a new life. When I thought you were lost to me, I had not courage to think of anything. But I will write to my friends out West and tell them I accept the nomination, and then I will see what one clear brain—what one earnest heart can do, for surely this great country with its vast and varied resources, with its strong race at once quick-witted and robust, nervous and energetic—surely this country is worthy of a better fate than to become the prey of rapacious speculators and greedy politicians, and the plaything of a grotesque collection of strutting mountebanks who are beginning to entitle themselves the upper-classes and who have neither the external refinements of an old civilization, nor the vital energies of a new one. No, surely, New York society is not the quintessence of American progress.

(Curtain.)